STONE GAME

A Stone Cold Thriller

J. D. WESTON

1

NOAH'S ARK

WHEN THE DOORS OF PENTONVILLE PRISON CLOSED behind Noah Finn and he smelled the fresh air, he knew that life on the outside would be harder than on the inside. At least while he was serving his time, guards could lock him in, and other inmates who preyed upon men like him could be kept away, as long as Noah played the game and reciprocated the good deed when the time came.

It had only been three years since he walked as a free man and nothing much had changed, except the sky was blue and cars were newer and more modern looking. On the inside, Noah had developed eyes in the back of his head. An almost sixth sense of situational awareness was the result of an extremely difficult first three months. He'd been beaten, raped and forced to do shocking things to other men with the point of a sharpened tool in his ear as motivation.

On the train to his old home in Dunmow, Essex, he found a seat at the far end of the carriage where he could see the other passengers and anyone who came in from the next carriage. He would be ready. Something else he'd learned; it wasn't good enough just to know where everybody was, he needed to be ready to defend himself whatever way he could.

He watched London slip by and give way to the green fields of the Essex countryside. It was the middle of the day and a few other passengers shared the journey with him. All of them were oblivious to the man who was sitting at the end of the carriage, and the terrible things he'd done.

Eventually, the train stopped in Chelmsford, where Noah disembarked and made his way to the bus station outside. It seemed an age since he'd been there, and he remembered it well, despite the local council's vain attempts to keep it looking fresh.

Standing waiting for the bus that would pass through his village of Dunmow, he felt vulnerable. He was aware of his appearance; his dirty old running shoes, tracksuit bottoms and an old leather jacket were all the clothes he had. His smarter jeans had been ruined on his first day inside when he'd been accidentally left alone with two other inmates. Maybe it had been a genuine mistake, but Noah thought otherwise. He knew it had been a chance for the guards to size him up, to see if he would be trouble, to see if he would fight back, cry or just take his punishment. Noah Finn had curled into a ball on the floor and taken the beating. He hadn't cried, it had all happened too fast; the tears had come when he was taken to his cell and left alone for the first time.

The bus arrived and Noah stepped on, glad to be somewhere relatively safe. He noted the cameras on the bus; they hadn't been there before he'd been away. It gave him a sense of security. He kept telling himself that he'd paid his penance, and he was now a free man. Yet he couldn't shake the feeling that society hadn't forgotten, and they never would.

The ride took thirty minutes, and Noah allowed himself a smile at the familiar sights. He made a plan. He'd pick up a few things from the store and then go home, where he'd stay for a few days. It would take that long to get his things together and his money sorted. Then he could leave, and go find somewhere he wouldn't be recognised. A new life was what he needed. A fresh start.

The bus stopped at the north end of the village, and Noah stepped onto the pavement. He habitually looked left and right and then behind him before he began walking at a brisk pace towards the big store halfway down the high street. He glanced over his shoulder and avoided eye contact with the few people he passed by looking into the shop windows. Thankfully, nobody recognised him.

He began to feel safer when he turned into his quiet street. His house was the third from the end, a semi-detached three-bedroom house that his parents had left him. A part of Noah was thankful that his parents were dead. They'd be destroyed by the shame. But part of him wished his mum was alive; he always felt safe with her. She had died a few years after his father, and as he walked along his street, he remembered how they'd sit together in the evenings. Noah had often been taunted by the local children for his appearance. He knew he had the look of a dummy, he knew his jaw hung open, and that his eyes were too close together. He knew his clothes weren't fashionable.

The kids had thrown stones at him and called him names. Some of it was because his parents were strict churchgoers and seemed to be stuck in the fifties or sixties. But he knew that he didn't help matters by the way he looked. One time, some boys had found him in the woods at the end of his street. It was the only place he could go to relieve himself when he got the urge. His parents wouldn't allow their son to molest himself in the house, and though he had his own room, their strong belief in God made him feel as if He was there, even though he secretly didn't believe himself. A stone had hit him on the back of his head, and he'd fallen over with his tracksuit bottoms around his ankles. That was when the taunting got really bad.

Noah's father woke up one morning to find the word 'wanker' sprayed across his old Ford Cortina, and people began to cross the street when Noah was walking towards them. Word had apparently spread around the small village.

Those boys would be adults now, thought Noah, as he pushed the gate of his house open and closed it behind him. He wondered if they would remember him, or if it would all be put down to childhood shenanigans. He wondered if they'd still call him 'Nobby Noah' if they saw him. He didn't know why he cared what they thought or if they'd remember him. None of it would matter in a few days.

But he knew three girls who would never forget. He also knew that three girls meant three families, brothers, fathers and mothers who would all know sooner or later that Noah had been released. If he could keep his head down for a few days until his money came through from the transfer, he would be okay.

He stepped through the overgrown garden to the familiar brown front door, which now had flaky paintwork and abusive insults sprayed across the small glass window at the top. He shut the door behind him and leaned back onto it. Closing his eyes, Noah took deep breaths. He was safe.

He pulled the small security chain across to its locked position and let his eyes wash across the large hallway. The parquet flooring was just as he remembered it, dirty and dusty, but exactly as it had been. The flowery wallpaper his father had hung was peeling in some of the corners, and a simple wooden statue of Jesus on a cross was fixed to the centre of the wall between the front door and the entrance to the living room.

The house was large with huge bay windows at the front and a great chimney breast in the living room. The journey and his emotions had got the better of him and, seeing the couches in the front room, he realised how exhausted he was. He tested the lights; the electricity was still on. The bills had been paid automatically from his account while he had been away.

He took a seat on the green couch and gently bounced twice, relishing the comfort. His mother's crocheted blanket hung over the back, just as Noah had left it. The TV wasn't a flash flat screen. It was big and boxy, and he had to stand to turn it on. He'd had a nicer TV in his cell, but not his mum's comfy green couch.

While he was up, he took his small bag of groceries to the kitchen. The huge butler sink was empty, and his mum's pans and cooking implements hung on the walls all around it. The old gas stove seemed to have an angry face due to the position of the knobs and handles. The pantry door was closed. Noah knew it would be a mess inside. He knew the perishable food would either be stale or already eaten by whatever rodents had got in, but there would be tinned food. With the addition of the few items he had in his bag, he would get by for a few days.

"Just a few days," he told himself, smelling the musty, stale scent of his old home. Beyond the kitchen was the small glass conservatory his father had built when Noah was a boy. He recalled how he wasn't allowed to help in case a piece of glass fell and cut him in half. He also remembered that the conservatory could be looked into from the forest at the end of the garden. He wouldn't go out there.

It was a light summer evening, and he'd had a long day, so Noah ventured upstairs. He was looking forward to changing out of the clothes from the prison. Most inmates had clothes brought in for them. But those who either didn't have anybody or couldn't afford it wore the clothes they came in with or whatever was left behind by previous inmates. Noah had been given a pair of old tracksuit bottoms, which he'd taken to the shower room with him to wash.

The old bath taps gave some resistance, but eventually, after coughing and spluttering, and an initial brown offering, they had produced clean water, and it was hot. He let the water run and walked to his old bedroom. The bed was unmade but everything was as he had left it three years earlier. It was a mess. The police had turned the place upside down. It was as if they had known where to look. They'd found the girls' underwear beneath his drawer inside the cabinet, but had turned the place upside down anyway.

He stepped over the mess and pulled out some clean clothes and a towel from his cupboard. Then he stripped, wrapped the towel around himself and headed back to the bathroom. The bath was halfway full when he stepped in, relishing the clean feel of the water and the hot steam cleansing his body. Showers inside had been sparse and brief or had been long and painful if he timed it wrong. He was pleased to sit in the water, and a small guilty smile crept onto his face as he laid his head back and put his arms on the bath edge.

That was Noah's mistake.

It was fifteen minutes later when he tried to turn the water off that he realised he couldn't move his arms. They were stuck to the bathtub. He panicked and tried to rip them off, but whatever held him there began to tear his skin. He kicked the tap off with his foot as his heart rate climbed and confusion set in. His skin was stuck by some kind of adhesive. But it was impossible.

Then he heard the voice outside the door.

2

NO ESCAPE

"ISN'T IT WONDERFUL?" SAID MELODY, STARING OUT OF the window of their rented campervan as Harvey coaxed it around the tight country lanes. "Don't you miss England?"

Harvey didn't reply at first. He finished taking the bend then straightened the van and selected fourth gear before he glanced across at Melody, who was sitting doe-eyed at the rolling fields and green trees.

"It's nice, yeah," replied Harvey eventually.

"Just *nice*?" asked Melody with a smile. "I love England at this time of year, the countryside and the rolling hills, the birds. It makes me wonder what life was like when things were simpler."

Harvey didn't reply.

"I love the colours in the grasses and the trees and the blue sky," said Melody. "I love the way the fields seem to join like a patchwork quilt that stretches on forever."

"Have you spoken to Reg?" asked Harvey. "You said you were going to call him to arrange meeting up."

Melody knew the romance of the scenery was beyond

Harvey, and she let the change in conversation go as easily as it had come.

"Yeah, I spoke to him yesterday. I *told* you I did," said Melody. "Don't you remember me saying?"

Harvey didn't reply.

"What *is* wrong with you?" asked Melody.

Harvey glanced across at her.

"Harvey, your silent, sultry demeanour won't work with me. Tell me what's wrong."

"Nothing's wrong, Melody. Tell me about Reg and dinner. Will Jess be there?"

Melody eyed Harvey, who purposely looked away and out of his own window.

"Yes, she'll be there. I'm looking forward to seeing them. It seems weird Reg having a girlfriend, doesn't it?"

"Are you going to give me directions?" asked Harvey.

Melody understood Harvey's tone. She knew not to push for an answer; it would come eventually, maybe when he was ready to talk.

"Just stay on this road and turn right at the end," replied Melody.

They drove on in silence. The glorious countryside around them overshadowed the fractious mood.

By the time they had reached the end of the long and winding lane, some thirty minutes later, the signs for Dunmow began to appear more frequently, and Harvey began to provoke conversation with Melody.

"So, this is where you grew up then, is it?" he said, seemingly impressed.

"Not far from here. We lived in the village, the campsite is close to our old house," said Melody. "I wouldn't mind taking a walk around there at some point to see the place."

Harvey didn't reply.

Instead, he turned a corner near an old cottage with a

huge thatched roof. The high street stretched out before them.

"So?" said Melody. "What do you think?"

"It's nice," said Harvey. "I like it."

"It used to be a lot smaller when mum and dad were younger, but it's such a pretty place. I think it still has most of its charm."

"Where are they buried?" asked Harvey.

"Not far, in the next village, we'll go there now."

"The *next village*?"

"Yeah, it's a stunning little place called Little Easton. They got married there too."

Harvey didn't reply.

"That's where I'd like to get married, Harvey, so mum and dad can be there. It's a beautiful church."

Melody watched for a reaction from the corner of her eye. Harvey slowed for a pedestrian crossing and turned to look at her, catching her sly stare.

"If that's what you want," he replied.

"You wouldn't mind?" she asked, surprised at how easy it had been to convince him.

"Why would I mind?"

"I don't know, maybe you had ideas of your own."

"I did," replied Harvey. "My idea was to get out of crime, move to France, ride my motorbike and sit on the beach for the rest of my life. And now look, I'm getting married to an MI6 operative, and we've got a dog and a bloody camper van."

Melody smiled and turned in her seat to see their dog, Boon, laying on his back on the couch at the rear of the camper. His ears pricked up and he lazily opened an eye. He closed it again and let his ear fall back flat, and Melody turned back to Harvey.

"Didn't think you'd get so lucky, did you?' she said

jokingly. "You *are* happy though, aren't you? You seem it. Turn right here."

Harvey took the turn. "I'm okay, Melody," he said. "I wouldn't change any of it, so don't worry."

"What's been your favourite part of the trip so far? Kent, the Lake District or Norfolk?"

"It's hard to say," replied Harvey. "The lakes, I think. I have memories of them all, but the lakes were peaceful and exactly how I remembered it."

A few minutes later, they came to a large church on the right-hand side of the narrow lane.

"Stop here," said Melody. "This is it. Do you see what I mean?"

"It's pretty," said Harvey as he stopped the camper opposite the old church.

Melody wasn't listening. She was already climbing out of the van and opening the door for Boon, who was pleased to see the old trees that lined the field.

"You want some time alone? You know, to go see your parents?" asked Harvey. "I'll keep an eye on Boon. We'll be by the lake down there." He gestured at the small lake that lie at the bottom of a hill.

"Thanks," said Melody. "I'll just be ten minutes at the most. Okay?"

"Take your time," Harvey replied.

Harvey watched Melody cross the lane and enter the small churchyard then he took a slow walk to a small road bridge that crossed over the lake beside the church. Boon followed, keen to stretch his legs.

Their trip had been perfect to date. It had been Melody's idea to take some time to see the country, and Harvey had agreed willingly but had wanted to stop at a few places, places he'd been in the past, in a previous life.

They'd spent a few days in Kent, and then a week in the Lake District, just walking and eating glorified pub food. Then they'd driven their camper over to the East Coast, and made their way down to Norfolk for another week, just enjoying the peace and quiet. Little Easton had been their next stop, and Dunmow, the village where Melody had grown up.

He was pleased to see her so relaxed and happy, which in itself, was a strange feeling for Harvey. Enjoying someone else's happiness was an odd sensation for him. He'd never been selfish, and deep down his moral compass was set true, but he'd never been close enough to someone to enjoy their happiness.

He was slowly coming around to the idea of being married. He still needed to officially propose, according to Melody. They'd discussed getting married briefly at the beach by their home in the south of France, and although he hadn't got down on one knee and proposed, Melody had seemed excited at the prospect.

Harvey had thought before about being married, and now for the first time in his life, he didn't have any objections. Married life would offer stability, some semblance of normality, which was a far cry to what Harvey's life had been so far. Maybe it was too much to ask, he thought. Maybe he'd done so many bad things that even marriage wouldn't bring a normal life, peace and quiet. It was almost immediately after they had been discussing the idea on the beach in France that they'd been approached by a man neither of them had seen before. The man had been serious when he'd offered Harvey work. He'd said that a man with Harvey's skills was hard to find.

Harvey had turned down the offer. He'd been lucky to live as long as he had, given the situations he'd found himself in.

Harvey had spent most of his life taking people out for his criminal foster father. It wasn't something he was proud of but he wasn't ashamed either. He'd killed more people than he remembered, and was grateful for the fact that he couldn't remember them. During his training, Harvey had honed his skills on the lowest members of society, paedophiles and sex offenders mostly. People that wouldn't be missed.

For much of Harvey's life, he'd sought the men that had raped and killed his sister, Hannah, when they'd been young. The sex offenders he murdered were his way of offering some kind of closure to Hannah, and the countless other girls that had been assaulted, had their families destroyed and suffered so severely. But once he'd eventually found Hannah's rapists, the need to target society's scum had ceased. Harvey had been able to move on, knowing that Hannah's memory could live in peace, even if she couldn't, and there was no longer a dark shadow hanging over her.

But recently, he'd been having dreams.

That's where the urges used to start, the urge to deliver suffering to those who deserved it. When the dreams started, Harvey would begin his hunt for a target. The internet had made it easier to find them. Offenders leaving prison or awaiting trial were easy targets. Old newspapers online or in libraries would give Harvey their backstories. Once he'd found a target worthy of suffering, he'd spend weeks researching them, following them, identifying their patterns and building a plan.

He was standing on the bridge looking over the lake. Large carp swam close to the water's surface, and the geese and ducks swam around them. He didn't want to start killing again, but the dreams were overbearing. They weren't too bad in the early stages, but if he didn't satisfy his urges, the dreams slowly became more intense until it was all he could think about.

He stared down at Boon who was watching the geese with a hunter's eye.

"How am I going to do it, boy?" he asked the dog. "How am I going to lead a normal life?"

Boon didn't respond. He didn't even look up at his master. The geese were far more interesting.

Harvey leaned on the side of the bridge and pulled a piece of wild grass that was growing close to his hand. He rolled it in his fingers mindlessly then flicked the little green ball into the water. The geese and ducks saw the movement and darted across to it, but a fish plucked it from the surface before they reached it. They were all too used to being hand fed, thought Harvey.

"Penny for them," said Melody as she approached the pair on the bridge.

Harvey turned sharply to her, snatched from deep thought.

"They're not worth a penny," he replied.

"What do you mean you're getting alerts, Tenant?" said Jackson. "You need to slow down and start making sense. You're running operations downstairs, and if the team see you flapping like this, you're going to lose your credibility. You need to stay strong."

Reg Tenant shuffled his feet.

"It was the old team, sir," he began.

"You mean Frank's team?" asked Jackson, long since bored of dealing with the repercussions of a dark ops team that he'd helped bring to a close.

"Yes, well, as you know, we were unofficially dark ops, and well, we did a lot of stuff that was very unofficial and-"

"Not quite legitimate?" suggested Jackson. "Is that what

you're trying to say, Tenant? You did things that bent the rules, but it was overlooked because the results were good. Am I right?"

"Yes, sir. We did what we had to."

"Tenant, I have a file on you all as thick as the Yellow Pages. I can assure you that everything you lot got up to was recorded and is safely tucked away. I personally refer to the files quite frequently so I wouldn't worry yourself about the records. But..." He pointed his index finger upwards. "I think we both know that Harvey Stone bent the rules a little more than most, and if someone *were* to look him up, it would probably raise a few eyebrows and take some explaining on his behalf."

"But, sir," said Reg, "that's just it. I knew the data was stored in a database so I ran some plugins that would send me alerts every time one of our names shows up in a search result."

Jackson cocked his head and began to listen intently.

He was sitting at his desk in his office in the Secret Intelligence Services building on London's Southbank and was responsible for a small covert operations team. He'd been recently promoted, which let Reg step up into Jackson's old role and run the operations as a team leader. Jackson merely steered the ship from the lofty heights of his office.

"I started receiving alerts, sir. Information was being pulled out about Harvey and what he did before he joined the team."

"Ah yes, Frank's data."

"Sir?"

"When your previous boss, Frank Carver, was '*killed in action*' shall we say," Jackson gestured inverted commas to accompany his statement, "we found the information on his laptop to be..." He searched for the right words. "Potentially useful."

"It was *you* who stored it, sir?"

"It *was*, Tenant. It was a department laptop, and the data was taken for analysis when Frank died."

"But now someone has found it, sir," said Reg. "Does that mean that Harvey will-"

"Get into trouble?" asked Jackson. "No, Tenant. Frank wasn't completely inept. He secured full exoneration for your friend Harvey Stone. But I must say, the charges would have been severe. Stone would be looking at something like two to three hundred years imprisonment."

"He's been cleared, sir?"

"Exonerated, Tenant," corrected Jackson. "I dare say some would have called to bring back the death penalty had the knowledge been made public."

"But nothing was proven, sir. Is that right? Besides, he even helped you get your promotion, didn't he?"

Jackson glared at Reg. He sat forward in his chair, raised his finger and lowered his voice.

"If you ever mention that incident again, Tenant," he said, "to me or especially to anybody else, it'll be the last thing you do in this organisation. Just forget any of it ever happened."

Reg took a step back.

"I'm sorry, sir, I didn't mean to bring it up."

"It was all based on Carver's notes," said Jackson, moving the conversation forward. "It was what he used to persuade Stone to join the team in the first place."

"The noose," said Reg under his breath.

"The what, Tenant?"

"Oh, err, nothing, sir. Thank you. Sorry to have troubled you." Reg turned and started towards the door. "One more thing, sir."

"Go on," said Jackson, leaning back in his chair and rolling a pen between his fingers.

"So, who would be looking for Harvey? Why would his

name come up in a search? It's a secure database, even I can't access it directly."

Jackson took a deep breath and let it out slowly. "Your friend Stone, Tenant," began Jackson, "upset quite a few people during his time with the force, even as an unofficial member of an unofficial team. He was wreaking havoc, as you know, and behind the scenes, Frank Carver was the puppet master pulling on every string he could find to stop Stone being carted away."

"Frank was *helping* him?" asked Reg.

"He was," said Jackson. "And once the exoneration was in place, there was little anyone could do but wait for him to do something else."

"That's entrapment, isn't it?" asked Reg.

"Not entrapment, Tenant," said Jackson. "He wasn't led into a situation where we knew what crimes he would commit. But we did know he would commit a crime eventually."

"But he's not in any trouble now, sir?"

"You're fond of him, aren't you?"

"He saved my life, sir. He saved all our lives on several occasions. But mostly, it's Melody, his-"

"Ah, Mills, yes," said Jackson. "She's a good friend?"

"She's the best, sir. I just worry for her. If Harvey is being investigated then she might be in trouble too."

"Reg," said Jackson, "I can assure you that, to my knowledge, Harvey Stone is not being investigated. It's probably just a random result. You're seeing them soon, aren't you? Did I hear you mention that a while ago?"

"Yes, sir. We're having dinner, the four of us."

"That'll be nice. Send my regards, won't you?"

"I will, sir." Reg opened the door and took a step. "Oh, and sir?"

Jackson raised his eyebrows.

"Thank you, sir."

3

SMALL SACRIFICE

"YOU CAN'T STAY IN YOUR CELL ALL DAY, TYSON," SAID
Prison Officer Grant. "Get yourself down to the showers and
clean up. You don't want your poor old dear smelling you
like that."

"I'm okay, thank you, sir," replied Tyson. "I'd like to carry
on reading my book."

"Tyson, I don't think you heard me. Get yourself down for
a shower. It wasn't an invitation," said Grant. "How long do
you have left?"

"Tomorrow, sir," said Tyson.

"The big day, eh?" said Grant. "Well, until tomorrow, you
still need to follow orders. Get yourself down to the showers
and clean yourself up. You stink. When was the last time you
showered?"

"A few days, sir. But I can wash here in the basin."

"Tyson," began Grant, "look, it's gym time. If you're
quick, you can get in and out before they finish."

Shaun Tyson put his book by his side and sat upright.
"Okay, sir," he said dejectedly.

He collected his prison-issue towel and a clean t-shirt

then stepped gingerly out onto Pentonville Prison's G-wing for vulnerable prisoners.

The showers were at the far end of the wing on the ground floor, so Tyson had to descend the mesh steel staircase, which clattered noisily. It was essentially a dinner bell for G-wing's less pleasant clientele.

Shaun kept as far from the open cell doors as he could as he made his way along the wing. He hated the walk. He hated the time of day, and he hated the prison. It was recreation time, and while others used the time to visit the gym, many didn't. They preferred to sit in their cells out of harm's way, or worse, waiting for someone like Shaun to walk past. Like a spider waiting for a fly.

G-Wing's vulnerable prisoners unit held a mixed bag of prisoners. While some, much like Shaun, were indeed vulnerable, fragile and ready to break at any given moment, other prisoners, more adapted to prison life, had found their way onto the wing and quickly established their place in the hierarchy.

It was these prisoners that Shaun feared.

He walked along the middle of the wing on the ground floor, kept his head down and moved fast. All the cell doors were open, but his peripheral vision kept watch for movement as he passed. He saw no movement. The concrete floor was painted grey with a gloss finish that the prisoners cleaned every day; to become a cleaner was a privilege you had to earn. Shaun had preferred to stay low during his three years inside. The cleaning duties gave prisoners access to all floors and they could ferry messages from prisoner to prisoner, which earned other less-formal privileges. Shaun needed no privileges. Shaun had been counting down the days since his arrival.

The showers consisted of an open wet room with a fixed bench to one side where prisoners could leave their clothes while they showered. Small partitions partially segregated each shower but offered little in the way of privacy.

As Prison Officer Grant had said, and to Shaun's delight, he found the shower room empty.

He gave a quick glance out of the door to make sure nobody was coming then pulled off his shirt and his prison-issue tracksuit bottoms as fast as he could. Then he darted under the shower, keeping his underwear on. In case someone came in and saw him, it offered a barrier of protection against the regular attacks.

The water was freezing at first but it soon became warm. It wasn't hot enough to soak under and relax, not like the shower at his mum's house, but it was just warm enough to wash under.

Shaun didn't particularly care about the temperature. Shower time was when he was at his most vulnerable. Shower time was when the spiders came out and the flies like Shaun found themselves trapped in sticky webs. Shower time was high alert.

He finished washing and pulled the water from his long, unkempt hair then quickly squeezed into his clean t-shirt.

Feeling pleased with himself for being so quick and not getting caught, he picked up his tracksuit bottoms and fumbled with the drawstring. He'd pulled them off in haste without untying them, and now the knot was stuck. He fumbled some more, but with wet hands, the job was frustrating.

"I hear you're leaving us?" said a voice from the door.

Shaun's worst fear.

He knew the voice; it was the one voice he'd been dreading to hear and had been so close to avoiding.

"Tyson," the voice said again, "I'm talking to you. It's rude to ignore somebody who's being nice to you. You know that, don't you?"

Pops Little liked to think of himself as the wing's father figure. The vulnerable prisoners unit needed someone like him for the inmates to go to with their problems. At least, that's the premise he used to befriend the younger and more vulnerable prisoners, like Shaun.

Pops Little was a predator.

Shaun had been caught in his web on his second day. He remembered it well. In fact, he'd never forget it. It had happened while everyone was working and Shaun hadn't been assigned a job yet. He'd been crying in his cell, adjusting to prison life, when Pops had walked by and seen him upset. He'd seemed so nice at first, and somehow, by using some kinds of psychiatric techniques, he'd coaxed a full confession from Shaun. Shaun had even cried on his shoulder. How stupid he'd been.

Shaun had been imprisoned for sex offences with a girl that had approached him while he was sitting in a park, which had then led to other girls recognising his picture in the local paper and coming forward with their own stories. But there were still more that hadn't come forward, and Shaun had told Pops all of them. It had been one of Shaun's biggest mistakes. Pops had threatened to use the information against Shaun and had forced him to do terrible things.

"Tomorrow," said Shaun, "I'm getting out."

"Good for you," said Pops. He had a thick wave of grey hair and features that one might think of when describing a generic grandfather, soft stubbly cheeks, glasses, a friendly smile, but hands as strong as any man's that Shaun had ever felt. "So, I guess this is goodbye then, Tyson?"

Shaun struggled with his tracksuit bottoms and decided to try to get them on without untying the knot.

"No need for that," said Pops. "Why not just pop them back down on the bench, eh? I think you owe me for helping you through your little spell here, don't you?" He shoved himself off the wall he'd been leaning on and made his way to Shaun.

"No, Pops," said Shaun weakly. "I just showered. I-"

"So, we'll shower again," said Pops smiling, "together."

Pops began to unbutton his jeans. "Come on, Shaun," he said, grinning. "One last time for old Pops. You'll miss me when you're gone." The old man grinned a yellow smirk.

Shaun closed his eyes. He couldn't bear to look at him anymore. He felt Pops grab his hand and pull it towards him.

"No, Pops," cried Shaun. "I don't want-"

"It's not about what *you* don't want, Shauny boy," hissed Pops. "It's about what *I do* want, and what *I know*, so if you want to go and breathe some fresh air tomorrow, if you *want* your freedom, you'll do what I say."

Shaun bit his lip and clenched his mouth shut.

"So get on your pretty little knees and say thank you to old Pops one last time."

"No," whimpered Shaun. "I can't do it." He began to sob. He squeezed his eyes closed but felt Pops forcing his hand open.

"That's it, Shauny," said Pops. He growled into Shaun's ear.

There was a dull thump.

Shaun opened his eyes to find Mr Grant standing with his baton in his hand. Pops fell limply to the floor between their feet. Shaun was terrified. He expected a beating from Grant, but instead, the prison officer nodded at the door.

"Get yourself dressed, Tyson," he said, "and get back to your cell."

"Yes, sir," said Shaun. He hopped on one leg as he pulled the tracksuit bottoms over his feet and squeezed them up to his waist.

"Sir," he called after Grant. "Sir?"

Grant was standing at the door, half in and half out of the

shower room. Shaun collected his clothes and towel and approached the much bigger man.

"Thank you, sir," said Shaun. "I just wanted to say thanks."

"Not my doing, Tyson," said Grant. "Warden said to keep an eye on you, so I am."

Pops moaned behind them and rolled onto his back on the wet and puddled floor.

"Get yourself back to your cell, Tyson," said Grant. "See if you can make it through the next twenty-four hours without getting into any more bother, eh?"

An old, bearded, drunk man bounced off the sickly, lime-green walls of the short, windowless corridor that led from the three interview rooms to the cells of Chelmsford Police Station.

Detective Chief Inspector Zack Harris stepped to one side to allow the homeless man and the escorting officer to pass. He was being released with no charge, free to go and piss up another shop front window the next night, and hope for another free night's stay in a cell sleeping on a sticky, blue plastic mattress. The whole transaction would cost the British tax-payer a few hundred pounds in labour, paperwork, admin and, of course, the inevitable deep cleanse of the cell once he'd left.

Harris continued along the corridor to the single desk at the end. He leaned over the counter and spoke to the deputy sergeant.

"Any free cells, Malc?" he asked.

"Hey, Zack," replied the officer. "Yeah, three and five are both free. Are you expecting a guest?"

"Probably, you remember Noah Finn?"

"Noah Finn?" said Malcolm. "The name rings a bell, but–"

"Nobby Noah?" said Harris, jogging his colleague's memory.

"Nobby Noah? Yeah, I remember him. Is he out already?"

"Skipped his parole meeting yesterday. Only two days out."

"Can't say I'm sorry, Zack," said Malc. "I'm not sure if society is ready for that nutter just yet."

Harris slapped his hand on the counter.

"I doubt very much that Pentonville is ready to have him back either, Malc." He turned and strode confidently back up the corridor and called back to Malc over his shoulder. "Catch ya later, Malc."

Harris buzzed himself through the thick security door that opened up into the rear car park, and then clicked his BMW unlocked. He'd arranged for a local squad car to meet him outside Finn's house and had told them to wait for him to arrive before knocking. Finn's house wasn't officially in Harris' area. But he'd been the arresting officer three years previously, and the powers that be thought a familiar face and knowledge of the previous case history might help ease any situation. Harris had dealt with skipped paroles before. Typically, the parolee was either adjusting and hadn't realised the penalties or, in the case of long-term vulnerable prisoners, they'd locked themselves away, too fearful to leave their homes.

The journey took twenty-five minutes, and the house was how Harris remembered it, in need of some TLC. There was the addition of abusive graffiti, and the garden that Mrs Finn had so lovingly tended had over-grown, but it still had the terrible brown door and old wooden windows.

Harris pulled up alongside the squad car, wound the window down and flashed his ID.

"Any sign of anyone?" he asked.

"None, sir," replied the officer. "Been here ten minutes now."

"Okay, look lively, boys. Let's get one of you round the back in case he makes a run for it. One of you stay in the car, and I'll take the front."

"Okay, sir," said the younger of the two officers, who was sitting in the passenger seat. He opened the door and made his way towards the footpath that led into the woods three doors down.

Harris parked his car, got out and locked it then headed to Finn's house. He caught the movement of a twitching curtain in the neighbour's house but ignored it, closed the gate behind him and walked to the front door. An old brass knocker took the centre position above an old brass letterbox.

Harris gave three hard knocks on the brass knocker.

He straightened his suit and tie then took a cursory glance through the bay window, keeping his suit jacket from touching the dirty old house. He couldn't see much, just some old tatty net curtains and a grim-looking living room.

He gave another knock then lifted the letterbox flap and bent down to peer inside. There was no sign of anyone, or even that anyone had been there recently. Just an old empty house. He stepped back to look up at the upstairs windows and saw the neighbour's curtain twitch once more. This time, he caught the lady's attention and gestured for her to come to the front door.

A few minutes later, long enough for the old lady to don her cardigan and shuffle through the house, the white PVC door opened a crack and her head peered into view.

"It's okay, I'm with the police," said Harris. He flashed her ID. "I'm looking for Mr Finn. Have you seen him recently?"

"Oh, I see," said the old lady. "You can't be too careful these days, you know." She opened up the door and stepped outside very gently onto her own garden path. "You're with the police then, are you?"

"Yes, ma'am," replied Harris. "I'm looking for Mr Finn. Have you seen him recently?"

"Oh, I see, in trouble, is he?"

"No, ma'am, no trouble. Just a few routine questions, that's all. Have you seen him in the past couple of days?"

"Have I seen him? Noah, you mean?"

"Yes, ma'am. I just need to ask him a few questions."

"Well, he hasn't been around for a while now. Poor fellow. I knew his parents, you know? Lovely, they were."

"I'm sure," said Harris. "When was the last time you saw him?"

"Well, that's the funny thing," she said, "I thought I saw him yesterday. Or was it the day before?"

Harris' head cocked to one side. Suddenly, he was getting somewhere. But slowly, very slowly.

"No, it was the day before," said the old lady. "I know because I'd just been to the shops. It's quieter during the week, you see, no children flying around on their bicycles and roller-whatsits."

"Ah, so you have seen him?" asked Harris.

"Seen him?" said the old lady with a confused look.

"Noah, ma'am, Noah Finn."

"Oh, little Noah. He was such a sweet little boy. My husband and I used to watch over him if Jack and Sue went out. He was only so big back then." She held her hand up waist high. "He *was* a pleasant lad though, *never* any trouble."

"And when was it you saw him?" asked Harris.

"I told you, it was the day before yesterday. I was watching the box, and well, not many people use this road, only the occasional dog walker going into the forest, so it usually catches my eye if somebody does, you know?" She leaned closer and whispered, "I like to keep an eye on things," then gave Harris a little wink.

"That's great. And what time might that have been?"

"Might what have been?"

"What time did you see Mr Finn, ma'am?"

"Oh, I see. Oh, I don't know, must've been early or late afternoon. Let me see, I watched the news, I always like to watch the news, my Harold used to watch the news, I must have picked it up from him."

"And then what did you do?"

"What did I do?" said the old lady. "Well, I watched the news then I took a little walk to the shop to get a few bits in for the week. I'd like to go to the big supermarket but there's no-one to take me now Harold is gone, and it's too far to walk, you see."

"So what time would you have got *back* from the shop?"

"Oh, I don't know. Maybe three o'clock?"

"And you saw Noah on the street?"

"No, I made a sandwich and I'd just settled down to watch that TV program with the two women, you know the one?"

"When you *saw* him?"

"Yes, dear. He walked up the path. I thought it was odd, but you know, I don't like to be nosy."

"Of course," said Harris with a smile. "Well, thank you, Mrs...?"

"You're welcome, dear," said the old lady. "Are you sure I can't get you a tea while you're waiting?"

"No, thank you, that's very kind. I have a busy day ahead."

Harris got the impression she wasn't going to go back inside her house, so he turned and gave the knocker another three raps before he bid her good day then walked back to the waiting squad car. The officer already had the window rolled down, and he smiled at Harris as he approached.

"She seems nice," he said.

Harris ignored the comment. "How's your mate getting on?"

The officer lowered his head and reached for the push-to-talk button on his radio handset. "One-one-nine, any action?"

The two men waited for him to reply. Harris straightened and looked up at the house. It was like time had been standing still in one particular spot and life had continued around it. The officer tried his colleague again.

"No reply, sir," said the officer in the car. "Want me to pop round and check on him? He might be in a dead spot."

Harris checked his watch and pushed off the car. "It's okay, I'll go," he said. "I could do with the walk. Keep an eye out here. No-one goes in or out."

The path into the woods was clear, as if the council had kept the route free of forest debris and the trees trimmed. But the bushes either side were thick and tangled. There was a small gap between the back fence of the last house on the street and the bushes, so Harris slid sideways into the space and made his way along, cursing at the damage to his newly polished shoes. The space widened out until it was large enough for him to walk normally, but he still had to duck under low branches and step over debris.

Small was nowhere to be seen. He wasn't in the trees and wasn't on the path. Harris gave Finn's back gate a gentle nudge. It was a six-foot high wooden panel with a curved top and black ironmongery. The gate swung open and Harris stared into the overgrown garden.

An apple tree took pride of place in the centre of what was probably a well-kept lawn back in the day. Harris judged it to be sixty feet in length. A carpet of rotten apples surrounded the base of the old tree. A small garden shed stood immediately to Harris' right; the padlock was intact. The shrubbery and bushes on either side of the stepping stone pathway leading from the gate to an old glass conservatory had grown out and onto the lawn, along with thick weeds.

Harris made his way slowly up the path, careful to step on the flagstones provided to avoid spoiling his shoes further. It wasn't until he was a few metres from the conservatory that he noticed a broken glass panel on the conservatory roof. It hung down precariously and Harris noticed that it was swinging softly as if a breeze was gently trying to wear its last functioning hinge away and bring the glass down with a smash.

Harris took a step onto the crazy-paved patio to have a look inside and then recoiled in shock.

Lying unconscious on the floor of the conservatory was Officer Small.

Harris reached for the conservatory door and wrenched it open, which released a length of string that had been fixed to the inside door handle. The string pinged away on its route around the room, pulled by some unknown force. Harris' eyes followed the string's movement, which finished at the hole in the glass ceiling.

He opened his mouth to call out. But it was too late.

The glass panel swung from its broken hinge for what seemed like a slow-motion eternity. Harris wanted to react. He wanted to move. He wanted to shout, but no words came.

All he could do was watch in horror as the sheet of glass that had been hanging so delicately from a single hinge broke free and fell vertically to the floor, severing Officer Small's head clean from his body.

4

STRANGE DAYS

HARVEY SAT BOLT UPRIGHT IN BED, WHICH WOKE BOON and Melody. The camper felt claustrophobic, and Harvey's sweat glistened on his chest. His arms ached as if he had been lifting weights and training, and his jaw hurt from grinding his teeth.

He pushed himself off the edge of the bed and pulled on his cargo pants and boots.

"It's dark," said Melody groggily. "Where are you off to?"

Harvey didn't reply.

He opened the door, let Boon jump down, excited at whatever was happening, and then stepped down onto the grass. He closed the camper door behind him and pulled on his plain white t-shirt.

A small picnic bench stood a few metres away so he climbed up, to sit on the table and put his feet on the wooden seat to tie his laces. Boon sprang from tree to tree to see who had tried to claim his territory while he'd been locked in the camper, occasionally glancing up at Harvey to make sure he was still there.

A short while later, the camper's rear door opened and

Melody stepped down holding two cups of coffee. Without saying anything, she walked over to Harvey, handed him a cup, and then plonked herself beside him.

Boon had completed his perimeter check and was idling back to his owners when Melody broke the silence.

"They're getting worse, aren't they?"

Harvey didn't reply.

"Why won't you talk to me, Harvey?"

Harvey looked away.

"I know, you know?"

"You know what, Melody?"

"The dreams, Harvey. I know you've been having dreams, and listen, you don't have to say anything, but if you want to talk about them, I'm here, okay?"

"How do you know about my dreams?"

"I sleep next to you, Harvey," replied Melody. "I know they're getting worse because they're getting more and more aggressive. You growl in your sleep."

Harvey looked across at her. He couldn't help but adore her. He hated her knowing about a weakness, but there was no getting away from it.

She growled playfully and leaned into him, linking her arm through his.

Harvey smiled.

"Thanks," he said.

"So you want to tell me about them? Do you remember them at all?"

"Vividly, Melody."

"Fact or fiction?" she asked.

"The dreams?" replied Harvey. "Fact. Old history, but undeniably, fact."

"You know what I think?"

Harvey didn't reply.

"I think you were exposed to some terrible things, Harvey.

What you saw when you were young would have broken most men. But you're different, you're resilient. What you did for your foster father had an impact on you."

"You don't understand."

"I understand enough to know that those things have a tendency to catch up with you. You killed people for a living, Harvey. No matter what way you paint that picture, it's always going to be ugly. You're a good man, Harvey Stone. Your conscience is dealing with the past. But it *is* the past. You have to *remember* it's the past."

She stroked the inside of his arm with her thumb and took a sip of the hot coffee.

"That's the old you. You left it all behind," Melody finished.

Harvey didn't reply. He took a sip of his own coffee then took a deep breath.

"I did some terrible things, Melody."

"I know, and the fact that I'm still here with you is a testament to how I feel about you, how everyone feels about you. You're a good man, you always have been, and people love you."

"I dream of the things I did. The faces, the pain. It's all there, it's all so real."

Melody was silent for a moment, then, "How long have you been having them?"

"All my life, Melody."

"I haven't seen you have them before, in your sleep, I mean."

"They come and go, like a calling."

"A calling?" said Melody.

Harvey didn't reply. She thought about his choice of words.

"In the past," she began, "when you had these dreams, you said they come and go. How did you stop them before?

Sleeping tablets? Music? I hear listening to music helps distract the mind."

Harvey didn't reply.

"We could try it?" she offered. "I'd be happy to have something classical on while we sleep. It might be soothing."

"It's a calling."

Melody stopped at the abruptness of Harvey's tone.

"You said that before, a calling to what?"

"An outlet. When I got them before, I'd go out and find someone." He stopped himself from saying too much.

"A girl?" said Melody. "You have me for that." She smiled and nudged him.

"No, not a girl," said Harvey. "Not that type of calling."

"Who then?" asked Melody. "Come on, there's nothing you can say that will shock me, Harvey. I've seen what you're capable of. What did you do?"

"The problem isn't what I did," said Harvey, "it's-"

"Go on," coaxed Melody.

Harvey sighed audibly and put his head in his hands.

"It's the way it makes me feel."

"How did it make you feel?"

"It's not normal, Melody," said Harvey. "I can't be right in the head."

"Are you saying you want to see someone? I can arrange it, confidentially I mean, no implications."

"I don't need to see a shrink, Melody."

"There's nothing to be ashamed about, Harvey. It's common. Even if you don't feel like you need to see one, you can go and they just keep you on track."

"Keep me on track?" snapped Harvey.

"Keep you-"

"Sane?" said Harvey. "Is that what you were going to say?"

Melody didn't reply.

"I'm not seeing a shrink."

"Okay, I just-"

"Well, thanks but no thanks. If I'm going to get through this, I'm going to do it the same way I overcome everything else in my life."

"So what's the problem?" asked Melody. "I mean, that's a great mindset to have, but if you really have such a strong mindset, what do you have to worry about?"

"I told you before."

"Tell me again," said Melody. "I'm trying to understand it. I want to support you."

"How it made me feel. That's the problem. At first, I did it to ease my tension, to feel like I was doing good. I did it because they deserved it."

"Retribution?"

"Yeah," replied Harvey. "I was helping the people that couldn't help themselves."

"But then?"

"But then it became something else."

"Like what?"

Harvey looked her in the eye.

"I enjoyed it, Melody."

"Malc?" said Harris.

"I thought you wanted one of my rooms?"

"That won't be necessary, mate," said Harris. "Things just got a bit lively here."

"Oh, okay. I'll take the reserved sign off the door and put the welcome mat away, shall I? Has he done a runner?"

"The exact opposite, mate, someone got at him," said Harris.

"Beat him up?" asked Malc. "How bad is he?"

"Dead, mate. Glued him to the bathtub with some kind of epoxy cement."

"Glue?"

"Yeah, you know the type that stays wet until it comes in contact with something?"

"What the-"

"I know," said Harris. "But whoever it was wasn't satisfied with that. The sick bastard cut his nuts off."

"They did what?"

"Then stuffed them in his mouth."

Malc took a second to digest the image. "Who'd do that to him?"

"It's a fairly long list, I'd say. There must be a few brothers and fathers out there who were just waiting for their chance."

"I guess you'll be busy interviewing then for a while?" asked Malc.

"I guess so, mate. There's a sicko out there that needs locking up."

"I'm speechless, Zack."

"And the worst thing about it was that Finn had probably learned his lesson but some twisted son of a bitch made him talk, probably wanted to hear him confess before he killed him. Imagine if it was your daughter that had been raped and the police had kept Finn out of your reach? You'd want to hear it from his mouth, right?"

"If I say yes, will you be interviewing *me*?" Malc joked, but immediately realised his insensitivity.

"Whoever our man is, he's disturbed, Malc. Finn's entrails were laying in his lap. His stomach was slit open. Doc reckons he was alive when it happened."

"Oh my-"

"That's not all. You're going to find out, so I might as well tell you," said Harris. "Our man set a trap up around the back of the house."

"A trap?" said Malc. "What for?"

"I took two of the Dunmow uniforms with me. One stayed in the car in case Finn did a runner, the other covered the back of the house."

"I don't like where this is going, Zack," said Malc.

"Sick bastard was there, Malc. He was just waiting for us."

"Go on," said Malc, not really wanting to hear what was next.

"He took out one of the uniforms, an Officer Small, cut his spinal cord and left him lying under a pane of glass."

Malc was silent for a moment, picturing the scene.

"The trap?" he said.

"I opened the door, Malc," said Harris. "It triggered the trap. The glass fell and took his head off."

Neither man spoke. They both knew the dangers of the job but it was rare that anything happened so close to home. In London maybe, but fifty miles out of the city in the countryside, life was tame in comparison.

"Sounds like the public is out for blood, Zack," said Malc.

"How do you mean?"

"There was something similar in Norfolk last week. Different setup but similar. Some guy was awaiting trial, some kiddy-fiddler or something, and the public got to him first. It was brutal, apparently. Took him into the woods and tortured him. Burned him alive eventually."

"Jeez," said Harris.

"You think it's connected?" said Malc.

"No mate, this was personal."

"So why did he kill our boy?" asked Malc.

"I asked myself the same thing," said Harris. "If he hadn't of killed Small, we'd have had to wait another twenty-four hours for the warrant. This guy wanted us to find Finn. Small was just a signpost."

"Somehow that makes it a whole lot worse," said Malc.

Harris didn't reply.

"Shout when you're free, Zack, if you need anything."

"Yeah, cheers, Malc."

Harris hung up the phone and relaxed back in his chair. He hadn't heard of the Norfolk killing, but then he hadn't really paid much attention to anything outside his own world for a few weeks.

He ran an internet search on the story before looking through the internal files. Often the publically available knowledge told the researcher a few more details that weren't always captured in an official police report, speculative details, opinions. Harris knew they couldn't be relied on as hard fact, but he wasn't looking for hard evidence, he was looking for a holistic view of the Norfolk incident.

He was looking for a link.

The internet search produced two pages of potential results, plus a few more details on the victim's backstory. Dennis Strange, a twenty-nine-year-old from King's Lynn in Norfolk on the East Coast of the British Isles, had been found by a dog walker in the early hours. The man had wished to remain anonymous and was being treated for shock.

Strange's body, or what remained of it, had its limbs mostly burned off before being dragged from the thick undergrowth onto the path as if the killer had wanted him to be found.

Strange, who had been awaiting his court appearance, had been reported missing two days previously. Many thought his disappearance had been an admission of guilt, but his parents had been adamant of his innocence. His body had been found on the day of his court appearance.

Harris checked the police report. There were no witnesses; nobody saw anything untoward. No tyre tracks, no fingerprints, no sign at all except a small fire, a pile of Strange's clothes and his ruined body.

"Practised," Harris said aloud to himself. "That isn't the scene of a first-time killer."

He was still waiting for the forensic report on Finn's house, but he knew already. There'd be no substantial evidence, not even the glass that had cut Small in two would be tainted. It was all too calculated.

"Who glues somebody to a bathtub?" said Harris aloud.

The killer had *wanted* the police to find the bodies. The cases were too similar not to be connected. What type of man goes to all the effort of taking someone somewhere private to torture them and then drags them back out to be found?

"Is he boasting?"

He picked up the telephone handset, dialled a three-digit extension and waited for it to be answered.

"Zack?"

"Malc, are you thirsty?"

"Thought you were busy?"

"I am, but I'm thirsty as well."

5

A LIGHT IN THE DARK

THE SHEEP'S HEAD PUB STOOD ON THE HIGH STREET AND was a busy lunchtime venue for the local businesses. A crowd of car salesmen from the nearby dealership were standing at one end of the bar, a few local tradesmen occupied the other end, and many of the tables positioned around the pub were busy with couples and colleagues deep in conversation. The pub did a good lunch, which brought in customers from all over town, and had done for years.

Harris was standing with Malc at the centre of the bar and ordered two ales.

"You okay, Zack?" asked Malc. "You seem a bit shaken up."

Harris reached out and took the first pint from the barman. He took a sip, and then set the glass down on a cardboard beer mat. He leaned down on his elbows. Then, as if agitated, he straightened and took another sip of his ale.

"I looked up that Norfolk case," he said quietly.

"Oh right," said Malc. "Gruesome, wasn't it? Burned the victim's arms and legs off in a bonfire. How does someone even think of that?"

"Yeah, it's sick, Malc."

"What's on your mind?"

"Doesn't it seem odd to you that both killers went to extreme lengths, *risky* lengths, in order for the bodies to be found? Finn's killer *killed* a policeman so that we'd find Finn, who was glued to the bathtub, so he probably couldn't place the body anywhere, and Strange's killer dragged him out onto a footpath several hundred feet away."

"What are you saying, Zack?"

Harris leaned with his back against the bar and one foot up on the brass footrest.

"Isn't it also odd that both murders were a little...?"

"A little what, Zack?"

"Out of the ordinary, Malc."

"Out of the ordinary, Zack?"

"Yeah, out of the ordinary," replied Harris. "When did you ever hear about someone being glued to a bathtub and having their entrails pulled out *while the victim was still alive?*"

"Yeah, that *is* a bit weird. But it takes all sorts, right?"

"And how about burning someone's limbs off one by one, again while the victim was still alive?"

"Okay, so they're both a little out of the ordinary, as you put it."

"And Small?" said Harris. "The killer took the time to set a trap for God's sake."

"Have you had the reports back yet?"

"No, they'll take time, but I just find it a little too coincidental. When I first read the Norfolk case, you know the first thing I thought?"

"Go on."

"Practised," said Harris. "Bloody practised. Who is practised at this type of thing?"

"Serial killers?" said Malc, unsure of where his old friend was going with the conversation.

"Yeah, sure, serial killers are one. But you know what struck me? What connected them both?"

"What, Zack?"

"Professional," said Harris. "Not just practised, but bloody professional."

"You mean they were hits? Contracted?"

"Maybe," replied Harris. He'd fallen into deep thought, so Malc left him to think and tried to enjoy his pint while he watched the football highlights on the TV.

A man and a woman entered the pub. Malc caught the eyes of the tradesmen follow the woman across the room. She wore a short, tight-fitting leather jacket with black leggings that showed off her lean figure. The man was of average build, dark hair, and had a dog on a lead, who sat down obediently as soon as the pair reached the bar.

"Do you have a lunch menu, please?" asked the woman to the barman. "I hear the food is still good here?"

She spoke clearly and confidently, and had no twangs of an accent. Malc tagged her as a local girl.

"I'll take the steak," said the man, without waiting for the menu. "Well done, side salad, mushroom sauce and a water."

"Make that two, please," said the woman, returning the unopened menu. "Shall we get a table?" she asked her companion.

Malc turned back to Harris. "You solved it yet?" he said, as he swallowed the remains of his pint and set the glass down on the wood.

Harris smiled weakly and finished his own pint.

"Let's go. I could stay here all day." He placed his glass on the beer mat, nodded thanks to the barman, and made towards the door. "I'm sure there's a connection, and if there is," said Harris, "he'll strike again."

"Well," said Malc, who was holding the door open, "you go catch him, and I'll lock him up for you."

Harvey took the table nearest the door and chose the chair with its back to the wall where he could see the entrance and the rest of the pub. He watched the two men leave and overheard a brief snippet of their conversation, which caught his attention. He continued to watch them walk from the pub door, through the car park and onto the pavement. One wore police-issue shoes, trousers and a white shirt under a long warm coat. The other wore beige pants, brown shoes and a similar long coat to his friend.

"Police?" asked Melody.

"Smell them a mile off," replied Harvey.

"Oy, you were one once."

"Unofficially," he grinned.

"I can't imagine what it would be like to be in the force around here. At least we were kept busy by serious crimes. Can you imagine having to go door to door, or investigating robberies and small crimes?"

"They probably say the same about London police, some people like the quiet life."

Melody smiled. She knew he was referring to himself, and his desire to just stop and relax.

"I was thinking about what you said," began Melody.

"Don't give it too much thought, Melody," replied Harvey. "I should never have told you."

"I *need* to know though, Harvey. I need to know the things that *affect* you. If I understand, I can be there or not. I can do whatever it is I need to do to help you through it. That might be talking or it might just mean I give you space. Whatever it is, I'll do it."

Harvey cut the sides off his steak, four perfectly straight cuts to form a square piece of meat. He cut the square in half and then cut the rectangles in half. He repeated the cuts with the smaller sections until he was left with four rough-edged fatty parts and sixteen smaller squares of meat, each a mouthful, and each of them small enough to fit into the little pot of mushroom sauce.

"The food has always been good here," said Melody, as she watched him prepare his food. "It's just one of those pubs, you know?"

"Yeah, we had a few pubs like that in East Ham back when I worked for John."

"I didn't take you for a *pub* type of guy," said Melody with a smirk.

"I'm not, but we'd have to go in and collect the protection, so we'd have lunch there too sometimes. Julios was a big eater."

"So protection rackets aren't all about beating up the owner and taking his money?"

Harvey grinned at the stereotype. "No, not at all. Most places were happy to pay us. They knew we kept them safe. That was one thing about John; he was fair. If a business paid, they had no trouble at all. He'd send the boys in at the slightest of bar fights. He pretty much owned them all in the end, all the pubs worth having anyway."

"Sounds dull," said Melody. "I mean surely you had better things to be doing?"

"I didn't mind it, nor did Julios. He thought of it as a familiarity check. It was a way to make sure he knew all the faces, and more importantly, to make sure they all knew him. Anyway, that's in the past. When are we meeting Reg?"

"I told him I'd call him. I thought we could leave the camper somewhere and catch the train into London?" replied Melody. "It'll be in Clapham somewhere. He said we could find somewhere to sit outside so Boon could come too."

Melody's phone began to vibrate in her pocket. She took it out, looked at the screen and saw the double zero number that Reg had used before, which meant a secure line. "Speak of the devil," she said.

"Reg?" asked Harvey with a raised brow.

Melody nodded and hit the green *connect* button.

"Hey Miss Mills, or should I say Mrs Stone?"

"Not yet, Reg." Melody smiled and reached across for Harvey's hand. "We were just talking about you."

Harvey pushed his chair back and indicated silently that he was going to use the washroom, leaving Melody to talk to Reg.

"So how's things? Where are we meeting?" asked Melody.

"All good, thanks. We thought we could go to the pub on the common. They're pretty cool about dogs in the garden, and I guessed you guys have done so much travelling in that old camper that you could do with a nice pub meal?"

"Yeah sure," said Melody. "Sounds good. Haven't had a pub meal for a while."

"Good, you'll love it," said Reg. "Where are you guys camping tonight?"

"Oh, Harvey wanted to go back to Theydon Bois tomorrow night. So we'll find somewhere local tonight. There's plenty of campsites and there's a place near Ongar my dad used to take us fishing. I'd like to go there just for old time's sake."

"Theydon Bois?" said Reg. "Why would Harvey want to go back there after what happened?"

"I'm not sure, Reg. I think he wants to see his parents' graves. We saw mine earlier."

Reg was silent.

"Reg?" said Melody. "What's up?"

"Nothing much probably," said Reg. "Listen, Melody, are you alone?"

"Yeah, Harvey has just gone somewhere. Why?" Melody's voice took on a serious tone.

"I just had an alert come through," said Reg, "from a secure database."

"So what? Surely you get those every day?"

"No, not like this, Melody. Someone's been looking into Harvey."

"What? Why?" she asked.

"I don't know, but listen, don't kill me for telling you this-"

"Reg, what's going on?"

"Apparently, Frank made records."

"Of what?"

"Of Harvey, Melody," said Reg. "He recorded everything he found out about him, everything Harvey told him, all the unsolved crimes that Frank put down to Harvey. Frank had been chasing Harvey for a long time, Melody. He didn't even know the extent of Harvey's crimes until he began to get more information from him."

"And he made this record? On a database?" said Melody, her voice higher than she intended.

"No. Frank's records were private. He stored them on his laptop. I doubt he meant for them to be seen by anyone else. But..." Reg sighed. "He probably didn't know he was going to be investigated and-"

"And what, Reg?" Melody asked. "Shot?"

"Well, I didn't want to go there, Melody, but yes."

"So when the old headquarters was shut down and Frank's laptop was confiscated, all the files were uploaded to a database for anyone with the right level of security to access. Am I hearing that correctly?"

"There's a strong security level, so it's not open to anyone, but yeah, someone with the right pay grade can see everything Frank had on Harvey. Basically, Frank managed to put together a list of unsolved crimes that fit Harvey's style, motivation and methodology."

"His noose?" said Melody. "You're talking about the noose that Frank had on Harvey all that time."

"Exactly, Melody."

"And now someone is accessing his files? Is he in trouble?"

"I don't know," replied Reg. "Jackson doesn't think so, but it's not my database. I don't have access to the SQL server. But I figured one of us might land in it one day, you know? For all the stuff that happened when we were on the team. So I ran a small plugin that would let me know if our names were called up in any searches."

"So it could just be random?" asked Melody. "What is it? A keyword search?"

"Well, not exactly," said Reg. "It's a search for similar cases. Whoever ran the search entered the details of a crime and pulled similar cases. Harvey's name popped up twice."

"And what was the search?" asked Melody. She closed her eyes in anticipation, unsure if she really wanted to know the answer.

"Well, we both know what Harvey did for John Cartwright."

"Reg, don't wrap it in fluff."

"Well, these are different. These are outright murders, Melody. They're not gang-related at all."

6

BEAST DREAMS

HARRIS WAS STANDING AT THE LONG WALL IN HIS OFFICE.
He stared at the photos that he'd stuck to his magnetic
whiteboard of Noah Finn, Officer Small, and the Norfolk
victim, Strange.

There was no apparent direct link between the crimes,
save for the location of the Finn and Small murders, and the
crimes that Finn and Strange had committed.

He pulled open the middle drawer of his filing cabinet and
found a folded and tattered ordinance survey map showing
the British Isles. Using a few small magnets, Harris fixed it to
one end of the magnetic board. Then, using a black marker,
he circled King's Lynn and Dunmow. The two locations
weren't too far to travel but were far enough to make the
journey purposeful. If it *was* the same killer, the murders
would need to be planned.

Harris used a red marker to mark the journey by road
using the A10, and a green marker to highlight the public
transport journey by bus and train.

He marked the journey times beside each coloured line.
The journey by road was fifteen minutes faster, not enough to

make a huge difference, which left both methods of travel open.

The door to Harris' office opened, and one of his researchers poked his head inside.

"Those reports you asked for, sir," he said, offering a blue folder.

"Thanks, George," said Harris. "Anything of interest in there?"

George held his gaze. "I think you should take a look, sir."

Harris caught the tension in George's voice. "Come in," he told him. "Take me through it."

A round, four-seater meeting table stood in the centre of the office. Harris cleared the surface of his files and allowed George to begin taking him through his findings.

"So, sir," he began, "let's look at this objectively. We identified that the Finn and Small murders were out of the ordinary, and by that I mean they were not your average gun to the head or throat sliced jobs, right?"

"Right," agreed Harris.

"Okay, so we ran a few searches to begin with to give us a pool of data. Homicides in the last week, month and year. There's a fair amount of data, so we narrowed that down to unsolveds and in progress, which narrowed the data down to a manageable amount."

"Good. How many are we talking about?" asked Harris.

"Still a couple of hundred, sir," replied Harris. "But after that, we removed all the gun crime and knife crime. This had a great result and left us with enough that we could then go through manually and remove any other run of the mill murders. The results speak for themselves, sir."

"Go on," said Harris. "Where does it leave us?"

"Three, sir," said George, "including the King's Lynn burning."

"Three?" said Harris. "In how many years?"

"One, sir," said George, "well, two weeks, actually."

"Two weeks?"

"Do you want to see them?" asked George, tentatively, as if he didn't actually want to see them himself.

Harris looked at the closed file with George's hand laid flat on top. "Open it up," he said.

George reluctantly opened the cardboard folder. Harris was met with a photo of a man who'd had his face peeled off. There had been an incision from the bridge of the nose to the nape of the neck, and the skin had been forced down revealing the skull.

"He has a taste for the extreme this one, George."

"Forensics results are a bit bizarre on this one," said George.

Harris tore his eyes away from the horrific photo and met George's.

"From the tissue they found beneath the guy's fingernails, the angle of the cut and the way the skin had been pulled down, they reckon he did it himself, sir."

"He did this to himself?" asked Harris, his eyebrows raised.

George nodded, unable to reply.

"Where was he found?"

"In a forest, sir. A small village near Canterbury."

"A small village you say?" asked Harris.

George nodded. "Yeah, Queensbridge I think, sir."

Harris turned to his map and found Canterbury.

"East of Canterbury, sir," said George, seeing what his boss was doing. The map of the British Isles was too high level to show small villages, so Harris circled the approximate area.

"Who was he?" asked Harris.

"Rimmell," said George. "Anthony Rimmell."

"Anything on him?" asked Harris.

George sighed. "He's on the list, sir."

"The list, George?"

"The sex offender registry. It-"

"It's okay, I know what that is," said Harris. "Had he served his time?"

"He was released a few years ago," said George. "Reports and statements from his neighbours state that he kept himself to himself, had a council job and lived a quiet life."

Harris pulled four magnets from the top corner of his board and stuck the new image below the Norfolk murder.

"Who's next?" he said to George.

"Elaine Stokes."

"A woman?" asked Harris.

George nodded. "Her body was found in the Lake District, in a-"

"Small village?" finished Harris.

"Little Broadwater, sir."

"On the-"

"Registry?" finished George. "Yes, sir. She served five years. Had a fetish for-"

"Spare me the details, George," said Harris.

"You want to see the photos?" asked George.

Harris nodded slowly.

George revealed the next photo. Elaine Stokes had been tied to a tree, her fingers had been severed, her tongue cut out, and her eyeballs removed.

"Post-mortem report suggests the victim was alive throughout the ordeal," said George.

"How did she die?" asked Harris. "Blood loss?"

"No, sir," said George. "Heart attack."

"I guess it all got too much for her," said Harris. "Any sign of-"

"Sexual interference, sir?" said George. "No."

Harris put the picture on the magnetic wall and marked the village location on the map.

"What dates do we have, George?" said Harris. "Let's see if we can understand this guy's travel patterns."

"Canterbury was ten days ago. Lake District was seven days ago. Norfolk was four days ago, and Dunmow was one day ago."

"Every three days?" said Harris. "Seems weird that the timings are consistent."

"Three days is easily long enough for somebody to get from one to the other by public transport, sir," said George.

"Hotels," said Harris. "Get onto them. I want the names of anyone who stayed in a hotel in those areas at those times cross-checked. Start with a five-mile radius then move out to ten. You know what to do."

"That's not the end of the report, sir," said George, making a note on his pad to check the hotels.

"There's more?" said Harris.

"I ran a search, sir, for similar methodologies, similar victims. You know, scratching at anything I could. I extended the time frame of the search."

"Go on," said Harris.

"Nine years ago, in a small village here in Essex, a dog walker found Roland Dyer dead in a forest."

Harris was intrigued with where George was going with the story and perched on the edge of his desk listening intently.

"He'd peeled his own face off, sir," said George. "Same cut, same everything."

"He's done it before?" said Harris. "The killer, I mean?"

"Seventeen years ago, Debbie Taylor was found tied to a tree in the middle of a field in Sussex."

Harris' eyes opened wide. "With her fingers, tongue and eyes removed?"

"Yes, sir, same methodology," said George. "But Elaine Stokes died of a heart attack; Debbie Taylor had to be finished off."

"Is there more?" asked Harris.

"Thirteen years ago, Eric Dove was found in East London with his limbs burned off. Just the charred stumps of his arms and legs and his brutally beaten torso."

"Any convictions for any of these?" said Harris, shaking his head in disgust.

George shook his head. "All of them in the unsolveds, sir. Essex police have a pile of files three feet high, all brutal murders, all victims were sex offenders, or at least on the list, and all of them unsolved."

"All in Essex?" asked Harris.

"Seem to be. Essex and East London anyway, and the surrounding counties."

"But these recent murders span the entire country?"

"Maybe he just passed his driving test, sir."

"Right," said Harris, ignoring George's poor taste in humour. He pushed himself off the desk. "Let's separate them. Two columns, old murders and new murders."

Harris began to re-arrange the victims on the magnetic board.

"When was the last of the old murders?"

"Two or three years ago," said George. "Some guy was found boiled to death in one of those old copper bathtubs like you see in the films."

"Boiled to death?" said Harris, disgusted at the thought.

George nodded.

"What the bloody hell are we dealing with here?"

"I don't know, sir, some kind of vigilante, I suppose."

"Boiled in a bath, George?" said Harris. "Was the victim on the list? I think I remember reading about that in the paper."

"*He* wasn't actually on the list, sir," said George. "But he was found in a basement with a known sex offender tied up beside him."

"Alive?" asked Harris.

"He's serving his time now," said George. "Pentonville Prison."

"Can we talk to him?' asked Harris.

"Not without a few questions being asked."

"Questions, George?"

"Like what exactly are we doing here? We're not exactly the right people for this job, are we? This is nationwide, sir. Government stuff."

"Yes, but the government aren't looking, are they?" asked Harris. "And *we* are. Right, here's what I want to see, a map beside this one with every one of those unsolveds on."

George nodded. "Easy."

"Then," continued Harris, "beside that, I want to see a list of the murders. Don't worry about the names of the victims. I want to see methodologies."

Harris began to pace. His mind was piecing the information together. "Two columns, new murders, old murders. Got that?"

"Yeah, we can do that," replied George.

"Put Elaine Stokes beside Debbie Taylor, Eric Dove beside the Norfolk guy, and Anthony Rimmell beside Roland Dyer. I think the killer is reliving his past. We should be left with a list of methodologies that he hasn't *re-enacted*."

"Right, sir. A list, sir," said George, making another note. "Got it."

"Then, get someone to do some research on known sex offenders already released, due to be released, or pending trial. Find the official sex offender registry, check the names on that, plus there's about a dozen unofficial lists online. Check the names on each list, discount any that do not contain the names of all the recent murders. Bring me the lists that do contain them. We may find the list that the killer is using to find his victims."

"Right, I get it, sir. So we'll have a map with all the old murders on, a list of methodologies, and a list of potential victims."

"Yeah, that's right," said Harris. "Hold on, George."

"Sir?"

"Noah Finn? Has the methodology been-"

"Edward Constable was found glued to his bathtub with his stomach slit open and his entrails on his lap," said George. He then took a deep breath. "They also found his testicles in his mouth. Eight years ago, sir."

Harris listened to the description and tried to fight the image forming in his mind.

"George, are you up for this?" asked Harris. "It could be quite a sensitive case."

"I'm game, sir," replied George. "But there's one thing I don't understand."

Harris looked across the room at him standing with his hands in his pockets and staring at the photos on the wall.

"Why would somebody be so vicious?" he asked. "I mean why go to these lengths to hurt these people? We're not just talking about murders; these people died slow and painful deaths."

"Easy," said Harris, turning back to the board, "suffering, George. He likes to make them suffer, just like their own victims."

George was silent in consideration, then asked, "But why?"

"Because *he's* suffered, George."

"I used to come here as a kid," said Melody, looking at the lazy river roll past and the trees blowing gently in the soft breeze. "Dad would bring us here for a day of fishing, so we'd wait for him to tire of us being too noisy then we'd head off into the trees. I do miss England, Harvey."

Harvey didn't reply. He stared at the water rolling past.

"You're keen to get back to France, aren't you?"

"I'm keen to get on with my life, Melody."

"Our lives, you mean?"

"Yeah."

"You don't sound so sure about that, Harvey."

"I'm just not used to doing nothing, Melody. I'm adjusting. I feel like I need a run. We've been cooped up in that van for two weeks now."

"We'll be home in a few days. Let's enjoy it while we can, and before you know it, you'll be running along the beach again."

Harvey didn't reply.

"Do you still want to go to Theydon Bois tomorrow? To see your parents' graves?"

Harvey nodded and laid back on the grass. The graves of his parents were unmarked and hidden in an orchard on his foster father's old estate. The visit would awaken many memories for Harvey.

Boon took Harvey's laying down as an invitation for him to move in for some attention, but Harvey held his hand low in a silent command, and Boon simply laid by his side.

"Do you mind if I head into town?" asked Melody, sensing Harvey's need to be alone. "The town centre is just a few miles away. I'll be gone a couple of hours."

"Fine by me," said Harvey. "I might take this dog for a run."

The pair said goodbye, and as Melody steered the big

vehicle onto the track that led from the trees to the main road, Harvey began to slow jog along the riverbank.

The run felt good, it always did, and soon, Harvey began to feel more like himself. He sprinted for a long flat stretch then slowed for a short burst between the trees. He found an old stone bridge and crossed over to hit a big hill that lay on the far side of the river.

Boon stayed at his heels the whole time, loving the exercise as much as his master. He would occasionally split off from Harvey to bound through the long grass or run through the shallows of the river, but his eyes never lost sight of Harvey.

With his arms pumping and his breathing in a locomotive-like rhythm, Harvey sprinted up the hill. At the top, he stopped and immediately stretched his muscles, taking in the view below him. A blend of yellow, brown and green fields lay in random patchwork formation across the landscape, broken only by the dark green lines of hedgerow and small pockets of trees. Melody was right; England was a beautiful place, he thought.

But England also held dark memories that Harvey would sooner forget.

The dreams had got worse since they had arrived in Essex. The memories were so much more alive. They had even passed a field the previous day where Harvey had once buried a man alive. The horrors of Harvey's life, the faces of the dead, and the guilty pleasure of killing were coming together at once, and there appeared to be no escape for him.

Harvey dropped down at the top of the hill. Boon slunk between his legs and curled up in the space.

"What's it all about, boy?" he asked Boon as if the dog could read his mind.

Boon looked up and nudged him, but Harvey didn't respond.

From where he was sitting, Harvey's view was unob-structed in almost every direction, save for the forests that ran beside the river. But inside, there were too many obstructions.

He laid back, enjoying the peace and quiet. The birds chirped and the breeze lightly rustled the grasses and the leaves in the trees. Boon curled into him, closed his eyes and soaked up the summer sun that warmed his face. Harvey's tired mind and the serenity of his surroundings soon carried him away into sleep.

Old memories began to come alive once more.

Flashes of visions and the terrible things he'd done were captured as if a bright light had frozen them in time and etched them onto a photographic film in his mind.

The face of the man he'd buried alive flashed once, just as Harvey was covering the last trace of his face with soil. He'd left a hosepipe in the man's mouth, to allow the sick pervert a few more agonising minutes of life while Harvey had filled the hole.

The flashed image of the man's face eased into the sick-ening memory. Harvey had finished with the shovel and covered all traces then slowly tightened the end of the hose, gradually restricting the man's air. Then he released the hose and heard a lengthy gasp, as the weight of the soil took its toll on the body below.

Harvey had put the excess hose flush in the ground so that passers-by wouldn't find it, and then he'd left the man to die a slow and painful death.

Boon's barking woke Harvey with a start. He sat bolt upright and wiped the sweat from his brow. His shirt was wet, and his breathing heavy from the vivid dreams.

Boon barked once more.

Harvey slowly recovered from his doze and rolled onto his side to find Boon sitting beside the corpse of a man who'd been pinned to the ground with wooden stakes through his wrists and ankles. He was crucified with his arms outstretched, like Jesus but with his throat cut.

Harvey dizzied. He remembered the scene. It was almost identical to one of his dreams, and to a previous kill.

He moved away, scurrying backwards on his hands and feet across the grass. But the ground was sticky. Blades of the fresh and lush green grass stuck to his bloodied hands.

His shirt too was spattered with red. Harvey recognised the spatter. It was horizontal and arced. The result of a sliced throat.

"Boon, come here," called Harvey, as the dog began to sniff the stiffening corpse. But Boon's ears flattened against his head. His tail dropped low, and he looked around him as if confused.

"Boon," said Harvey. "Here, boy."

The dog eyed him with caution.

Harvey rolled and stood up, but Boon bolted away down the hill. He looked back briefly and saw Harvey chasing after him, so the dog picked up speed.

Harvey tore across the bridge after the panicked Boon and narrowly missed a small family who were out enjoying the sunshine, walking the path along the riverside. Boon was gone, and the family gathered behind the father, who stretched his arms out like he was protecting them.

Harvey stared at his sticky hands again then back at the family, and down at his bloodied shirt.

"Your phones," said Harvey. "Put your phones on the ground, one at a time."

"Get away from us," said the man, his arms outstretched behind him holding his daughter and his wife.

"Throw your phones on the ground, and I'll leave you alone."

Two phones landed beside each other in the grass.

Harvey stared as if waiting for a third.

"She doesn't have a phone," said the man. "She's too young. Take them and go."

Harvey bent to collect the two phones, and then tossed them in the river.

"It's not what it looks like," he said.

"Please leave us alone. We don't care what it looks like."

The sound of Melody arriving in the motorhome and honking the horn distracted Harvey. He turned back to see Boon jumping up at the driver's door to reach Melody.

"Go," he told the family without turning. "Leave, now."

7

DARK DAYS

MELODY PARKED THE CAMPER IN A SUPERMARKET CAR PARK and relaxed back into the seat. She pulled her phone from her pocket, found the recently dialled numbers and hit Reg's name.

He answered after one ring.

"Melody," he said, "how did I know you'd be calling?"

"Something's wrong, Reg," she said.

Reg knew that when Melody omitted the pleasantries, trouble was afoot.

"Talk to me, Melody. What's up?"

"He's acting weird. He's quiet, like something's on his mind."

"Isn't he always like that?" asked Reg.

"This is different. Something's very wrong. And I can't help thinking about what you said."

"We've been running our own investigation here," said Reg. "Jess and I-"

"What did you find?" asked Melody, cutting him off. She'd known he wouldn't be able to help himself. He was one of the best researchers she'd ever come across; if there was something to be found, Reg would find it.

"Remember I told you about that search?" he asked.

"Yes, it's all I can think of, Reg."

"So it turns out that some detective in Essex somewhere has entered the information of a few recent murders, brutal killings, Melody, and the search has flagged previous similar murders, all unsolved crimes."

"So?" said Melody.

"Identical murders that were carried out by none other than-"

"Harvey? No, it can't be true, Reg."

"Hey, I'm not making any allegations here. I'm just-"

"I know, I know, but I can prove it wasn't him."

"Have you been with him the entire time, Melody?"

"Well no, of course not, but a lot of the time."

"And where exactly is it you've been?" asked Reg.

"Are you questioning me, Reg?"

"No, Melody, I'm helping you," said Reg. "What route have you taken on your travels in the past couple of weeks?"

"We came from France," said Melody, "into Dover, and then up to the lakes."

"Did you stop along the way?"

"Of course we stopped, we're on holiday, enjoying the peaceful countryside."

"Okay, Melody answer me this, did you stop in a little village called Queensbridge, just outside Canterbury?"

Melody was silent for a few seconds then, "How did you know that?"

"Just a hunch, Melody," he replied. "Then you went to the Lake District?"

"Yes, we stayed for a while. We moved about a little, did some hiking."

"Did you go and stay in the village of Little Broadwater?"

"What are you getting at, Reg? You're scaring me," said Melody.

"Little Broadwater, Melody. Did you stay there or not?"

"Yes, we did. But nobody's ever heard of it. We found a little campsite and parked up. How did you know?"

"And, from there, you drove across to Norfolk?"

"Reg, stop it," snapped Melody. "Just tell me what you know."

Reg took a deep breath of air. "Melody, about ten days ago, a man was found brutally murdered in the village of Queensbridge, outside Canterbury."

"No," said Melody. "*That's* where we were."

"There's more," said Reg.

"Go on then."

"A week ago, a woman was found murdered in a forest in Little Broadwater. A couple of hikers stumbled on her body, what was left of it."

"Reg, stop."

"And last week," Reg continued, "a man was found in King's Lynn, Norfolk, with his arms and legs burned off."

"Reg, no more," cried Melody. "I said stop."

"You need to hear this, Melody. You *need* to know the truth."

"I can't *handle* the truth, Reg. It can't be-"

"Yesterday, a man was found glued to his bathtub in Dunmow. He had his gut slashed open, and his balls cut off and stuffed in his mouth."

Melody began to sob. She couldn't reply.

"Get yourself out of there, Melody."

"It *can't* be him," she said. Her voice whined as she fought to hold back more tears.

"I'm sorry, Melody," said Reg. "The database pulled out unsolved crimes then the results were whittled down to disregard shootings, stabbings, and what you and I might regard as ordinary murders. The data they fed in was matched and every one of the results was nearly identical to the records that Frank made of Harvey's old crimes. Luckily, the database did not match Harvey's name, just the crimes that Frank tagged as potentially his."

"But he was pardoned. He can't be found guilty of those crimes now, surely. Even if they did match his name."

"He was exonerated, Melody, for the older crimes. But these recent crimes?" Reg paused and searched for the words. "They're his style. He might as well have signed them. If Frank was here, he'd called it the methodology. They have Harvey written all over them."

"But why?" asked Melody. "Why would he need to do any of this?"

"Every one of these victims was on the sex-offenders list, Melody."

"The recent victims?" she asked.

"Old and new," said Reg. "They're not just common in methodology. They have the same motivation."

"And Harvey had the means," said Melody.

"Now," said Reg, "what are you going to do?"

"What *can* I do? I'm marrying a *murderer*," said Melody.

"Melody, come on. We all knew he was troubled. Come and stay with us. You'll be safe here."

"Safe?" said Melody. "You think *you're* safe?"

Reg didn't respond.

"*None* of us are safe, Reg," said Melody. "If Harvey knows that we know, that's it, game over for you and game over for me."

"You think he'd go that far?"

"He spoke to me the other night, Reg," said Melody, calmly and with the unemotional, flat tone of acceptance. "He told me he'd been having dreams."

"Dreams?"

"Yeah, but that was it. It's not like he's sleepwalking and doing this. But he woke in the night, he was upset, so we talked."

"And?" prompted Reg.

"He said he..."

"He said what, Melody?"

Melody was silent.

"Melody?"

"He told me he enjoyed it."

"George, let's go," said Harris. "There's been another one. Meet me downstairs."

He let the door close and took the two flights of stairs to the ground floor.

"Ground units are already on site, sir," said a female officer behind the central desk of the police station as Harris approached. She handed him a sheet of paper. "One body, male, early twenties. Sounds like he had his throat cut."

"Forensics?" asked Harris.

"En-route," came the reply. "Uniforms are already on site closing the crime scene down."

George came bounding down the stairs and joined Harris.

"Ready for this?" Harris asked.

George nodded softly then followed Harris through the door to the station car park.

"If it's him, he's close," said Harris as he pulled his BMW onto the high street, "and if he's close, we can nail him."

"Do we have a description?" asked George, scanning the report Harris had given him. "Who called it in?"

"Some bloke out for a walk with his family made a call about a strange man running after a dog with blood over his shirt and on his hands."

"And who found the body?"

"A couple of kids out playing in the forest." Harris breathed out loudly through his teeth. "They'll need a bit of therapy after this."

"How did he die?" asked George, flicking through his notes.

"He had his throat slit, according to the report."

A cog clicked in George's brain.

"Was he pinned down with stakes through his wrists?" he asked.

"I don't know. Read the report," said Harris.

George began to compare the report against his own notes.

"Jesus, it's the same," he said finally. "Benjamin Green from Southend-on-Sea. Released from prison for sex offences, and found three days later pinned to the ground in a forest with stakes through his wrists and ankles. That was five years ago." He continued to flick through the notes. "It says here that his throat was cut and he drowned slowly in his own blood. The killer was never caught."

Harris indicated and put his foot down. The BMW shot past the traffic that had slowed for the traffic lights and into the wide country lane ahead.

They found the crime scene a few minutes later. The road had been cordoned off, and the entry to a small picnic spot was awash with glaring blue flashing lights atop local squad cars.

An officer was taking statements from a few cars parked to the side of the road, a workman in his unmarked van, a family in a large car, and a woman with her dog in a camper van.

Harris slowed for a police officer to lift the red and white tape over his car as he passed under. He nodded his thanks before stopping on the shoulder of the empty road.

Ten minutes later, they were both looking down at the body.

"See how neatly the stakes have been carved?" said Harris. "It's like he selected the branches and took time to carve them."

"So he was planning this?' asked George.

"Either planning or watching and waiting," replied Harris. He looked about him. They were standing at the top of a small hill. A river cut through the ground below them, and a small forest blocked the view to their right. Long grass grew wild and free around the edges of the hill, but the middle was soft, lush grass, recently mowed by the local council.

"There," said Harris, pointing to a spot a few meters from the body. "Something's flattened the grass. It looks as if somebody laid there."

"Why would they lay beside someone they just killed?" asked George.

"Tell me more about the victim," said Harris, ignoring the question. "Was he on the list?"

"Actually, no, sir," said George. "No previous, no history of anything. He was a local boy."

"So why *him*?" asked Harris to himself. "Why change the motivation now?"

The sound of an approaching helicopter drew near then faded as the police chopper flew in concentric circles around the area.

A police photographer waited patiently nearby to photograph the scene before the body was removed. A hundred yards away, a few locals were being held back by uniformed police. A couple of boys with a football had obviously seen the action and come to see what was happening.

"Are you waiting for us to leave?" called Harris to the photographer.

"Take your time, sir," said the man. "He's not going anywhere fast."

"Can you get a shot of the grass there?" Harris pointed to the flattened spot that lay a few meters away.

"Yeah, no problem," said the man as he came closer.

"Get a tape measure on it too. I want to know how tall the person was who lay there," said Harris. "Let's go digging, George." He walked off towards the few locals that were standing behind the red and white tape a hundred yards away.

He was met with a greeting nod from the uniformed policeman and then he approached the boys with the ball.

"Hi boys. Any of you know who that is?" Harris said, pointing up the hill.

"That's Liam, mate," said the boy with the ball, a ginger-haired kid with a face full of freckles.

"Last name?" asked George, making a note on his pad.

"Liam Charlton."

"You knew him?" asked Harris.

"Come on, boss. They're just kids," urged George. He was not keen to get a bunch of underage kids involved in a police investigation without their parents' consent. The backlash would be unbearable.

"It's okay, mate," said the ginger kid. "Yeah we knew him, but he's a bit of a loner."

"Is he okay, mister?" asked another kid beside him, a smaller boy with a mass of shiny brown hair and two missing front teeth.

"No, sonny," said Harris. "He's *far* from okay."

"Right, that's enough," said George. "Thank you, boys, on your way now." He pulled Harris' arm and led him away. "What are you trying to do, land yourself a court case?"

"They're just boys, George," said Harris. "They know more than you think. They've see worse in films these days."

"That's right, sir, they're just boys, and they don't have

their parents with them. So anything they say that you try and use as evidence won't stand up in court anyway."

"Stop fretting, George," said Harris, taking one more glance at the body, the trees and the river. "Why don't you make yourself useful and go find out what the uniforms found out on the roadside."

Harris began to walk down the hill to the river.

"And what about you, sir?" George called after him.

"It's a bit hot, George," said Harris over his shoulder. "I might soak my feet in the river."

8

RELEASE THE MONSTER

MELODY PARKED THE CAMPER IN THE PICNIC AREA WHERE she'd left Harvey and Boon. Movement in the corner of her eye caught Boon tearing along the path up to the van. He jumped up and pawed at the windows for Melody, so she opened the driver's door and let him in. Instead of jumping across to the passenger seat as he usually did, Boon was sitting on Melody's lap with his ears pinned down flat as if he'd been naughty.

Melody searched through the windscreen for Harvey and saw him a hundred feet away standing beside the bridge. Even from afar, Melody could see his hands and arms were bloodied and hung loosely by his side. His white t-shirt had a red stripe across the front. The tone of his gaze was the eerie stone cold look that Harvey was known for.

Sirens sounded in the distance, and the whomp of an approaching helicopter grew closer.

Melody's eyes locked onto Harvey's.

She shook her head.

"No," she said disbelievingly. "No, you can't have." Melody

looked harder at the blood on his hands and up his arms. It was as if he'd butchered somebody.

The sirens grew louder and the helicopter began to creep into view from the far fields. Melody chanced a glance up into the sky and behind her to see if the police had arrived. But when she looked back, Harvey had gone.

Melody's mouth hung open. It couldn't be possible. What had he done?

The sirens were fast approaching now, so Melody turned around in the car park. She hovered by the exit for a moment, half expecting to see Harvey run from the trees and climb into the van as he'd done when they worked together. But this time he didn't appear.

"Is this goodbye, Harvey Stone?" she said softly to the rearview mirror, and then slowly pulled out of the car park onto the road.

She was stopped fifty yards later by one of two police cars that had been tearing down the hill from the town centre. The first car drove past, and the second stopped to let an officer out before parking across the road to stop any traffic from passing.

The officer on foot guided Melody to the side of the road, and soon after, stopped a family in their MPV and a man in a plain white van.

Melody knew the game. She'd wait in the camper for the officer to get to her. The others would climb out of their cars and become aggressive with the officer for delaying them. He would then make them wait longer.

Her mind spun at dizzying speeds. What had Harvey done? Was Reg right? Was Harvey was up to his old tricks again? She felt the dull stab of loss in her heart, and her breathing quickened. She cracked the driver's window ajar and rested her head on the steering wheel.

"You okay, miss?" said the officer who was standing beside the camper.

Melody didn't react.

The officer tapped on the window, and Boon began a low, menacing growl.

Melody straightened. She stared ahead and composed herself. Then she lowered the window.

"I'm afraid I'm going to have to ask you to step out of the vehicle, ma'am," said the officer. He then turned away and spoke into his shoulder-mounted radio.

Melody opened the door, moved Boon off into the passenger seat, and dropped down to the ground. She held onto the door for balance. Her head still spun with the suddenness of it all. Thirty minutes ago, she'd heard that the man she loved might be a serial killer; that news had been bad enough. But she had been able to defend him, even if not wholeheartedly. But now she'd seen the blood on his hands, and how shaken Boon was. Then the look on Harvey's face had confirmed her darkest thoughts.

"Ma'am?" said the officer. "Are you okay? You look shaken."

Melody looked despondently at the officer's uniform, from his polished boots to his immaculately pressed trousers and shirt, to his shiny shoulder IDs.

"Ma'am?" he said again.

"I'm fine. I just need a minute."

"Can I ask you what you're doing out here?" he asked.

Melody heard his voice but was lost in her own world. She imagined Harvey killing a faceless victim, his control and calm making the job seem effortless, his stone cold gaze watching with evident joy at the suffering he was causing.

"I need to know what you're doing here," said the officer.

Melody snapped out of it and focused on the officer once more.

"I'm walking my dog. I *was* walking my dog," Melody corrected herself.

"Have you had some bad news?" asked the officer. "Would you like a female officer to talk to you?"

"No," she said, "no need." She took a deep breath. "What's wrong anyway?"

"Who said anything was wrong?" said the officer.

"I sensed something was wrong when you and your mates came tearing down here and pulled me over," said Melody. "I'm on the force. Well, I used to be anyway." She offered a weak smile.

"You're not anymore?" asked the officer, suddenly interested.

"Special Intelligence," said Melody.

"Oh, I see," said the officer. "Well, if I could just take your details, I'll see about getting you on your way."

Melody gave the young officer her details and waited while he ran a check on her name and the plate number.

While he was gone, Melody watched as two plainclothes detectives arrived in a BMW. Melody knew the look, the car, the authoritative presence.

Were those the men that ran the database search?

She watched with interest as the two men parked, walked across the bridge and up the hill. Melody saw for the first time the red and white taped off area, a body under a sheet, and a few nosy locals who wanted in on the action. She gazed into the trees and wondered if Harvey was watching her, watching them, or had made his escape.

She hoped for one last glimpse of him.

A small part of her hoped that he'd escaped, while another part of her wanted him to be caught and locked up so he could do no more harm. But a large part of her didn't want one or the other. It just wanted them both to be back in the little farmhouse in France, waking up to coffee, making love and spending the day on their little beach.

"What a nightmare," she said to herself.

"What's a nightmare, Miss Mills?" asked the officer who had returned to the camper. "Are you sure you're okay? I can get you something if you want."

"Am I free to go?" she asked, ignoring his offer of help.

He nodded. "But don't go too far if you don't mind, Miss Mills. We may need some more details."

"I thought you said nothing happened?" she said to the young man. "So what would you question me about?"

"You know how it is, Miss Mills," he replied. "We may uncover a development." He smiled as if his answer had been a smart reply.

Melody climbed back into the van and started the engine. She leaned out of the window. "Let's hope for your sake that whoever is under that sheet up there doesn't need your help, Officer." She winked and pulled onto the road, leaving the policeman wondering if she just complimented him or insulted him.

Shaun heard the gates of Pentonville Prison close behind him. He clutched a plastic bag with his few possessions and walked timidly away from three years of hell.

He'd been given a small map and directions from the prison administration, but he pocketed the map and chose to just walk. He just wanted to be away from the place.

He felt eyes bore into him, as they had for the past three years. Everything he'd done had been seen, and everything he'd said had been heard. In prison, privacy was a luxury that was forfeited. He felt like the people he passed on the streets all knew where he'd been, and worse, he felt as if they all knew why he'd been sent there in the first place.

He kept his head down and walked.

Shaun found Caledonian Road, a busy street that allowed him to fall in with the other pedestrians, people who ignored him. He relished the feeling of being ignored, of being alone on the outside; it somehow made him feel part of something.

Shaun thought it bizarre how he felt included in something where people ignored him, ignored everyone else around them, and all had places to go in a hurry. He pulled the map from his pocket and studied it as a tourist might. He decided he'd walk to Hornsey Station. From there, he could take a train directly to his mum's house. The walk ended up taking more than an hour, but Shaun didn't mind. By the time he reached the train station, some semblance of normality had kicked in.

Life on the outside.

The train ride to Potters Bar was a welcome break. The carriage had been empty, and the seats were softer than his prison bunk had been.

He lifted his feet up onto the seat in front, only to remove them when somebody else boarded the train at the next stop. It would take a while, he thought, to get over the fear.

He tried to remember his mum's house and wondered if it had changed. He'd told her not to visit him after the first time when she'd broken down. He couldn't face putting her through the agonising turmoil of visiting again. But when he'd earned enough money to pay for his weekly TV privilege and his tea each week, he'd spent whatever else he had on calls to her.

It had been easier that way.

He thought of Pops, who had been sitting in the visiting room not far away during Shaun's mum's first and only visit, the look in his eye, those thin, cruel lips, and the knowing wink he'd offered as Shaun consoled his crying mum.

Shaun had broken first, and that had set his mum off. It was a common sight in prison, and most prisoners ignored the emotions of others. Everybody felt it, the missing, the shame, the guilt and the heart-wrenching agony of watching a loved one sit across the table wondering why you did what you did. It wasn't just the prisoners that suffered, it was the lives of those around them that were destroyed.

An unexpected and overwhelming feeling of claustro-phobia kicked in when Shaun stepped out of Potters Bar Train Station. He couldn't be sure if it was because of the familiarity of the buildings and the layout of the town, or just plain old paranoia, but the feeling returned with a vengeance. It was as if every person he passed on the street eyed him with suspicion and knowing. Heads turned in the cars that drove by as he crossed the main road into the quiet side streets. But somehow, instead of getting away from the stares, the secluded roads offered the few passers-by more time to study him, to remember him.

The weird kid who fiddled with young girls.

Shaun began to run. He took to the alleyways that ran between the streets behind the rows of houses until he came out onto his mum's road. From there, he dropped his pace to a brisk walk and kept his head down until the sanctuary of his mother's garden path fell into his field of vision. He fumbled with the gate at first, and then the front door key in his sweaty palm, which had been one of his possessions the prison administration had taken.

He failed to notice the light blue Ford parked a few houses down and the man with the digital camera and tele-photo lens.

Shaun quickly slammed the front door behind him. He hadn't meant to; it just closed quicker than he expected. He put his back against the door and rested his head on the wood to regain his composure. Then, hearing his mum in the kitchen, he pushed off the wall and opened the kitchen door.

Shaun's mum had been waiting for him. She was sitting at the small square kitchen table with a cup of tea in one hand and a cigarette in the other. An overflowing ashtray on the tablemat was evidence of how she'd spent the morning.

There was a long silence as mother and son exchanged looks of mixed emotions.

"Oh, Shaun," said Mrs Tyson, and then burst into tears.

Shaun bent and hugged her, and buried his face in her hug.

"I'm home, Mum," he said. "I'm not back there again. I promise"

Mrs Tyson pulled away, composed herself, and wiped her eyes.

"It's good to see you home, Shaun," she said. "Are you hungry?"

"Erm, no, Mum," he replied. "Not really."

"What have you had to eat?"

"Nothing, Mum," said Shaun. "I just couldn't stomach anything."

"Well you *must* eat," said Mrs Tyson. "I've got some bacon and some bread, and later I'll go to the store. What do you want for dinner? My treat."

"Oh, Mum," he said, "you don't have to do that."

"I know I don't *have* to, Shaun, but I *want* to. I want to cook you a nice dinner. What was the food like? Did they feed you well enough? You look like you lost weight."

"I'm okay, Mum, honest."

"Well, I'll do a roast," said Mrs Tyson with finality. "How about a bit of beef with all the trimmings, eh? Then we can sit, and you can tell me all about what you're going to do now you're out. We need to put all this behind us and move on."

She began to dry a dish that was already dry and had been sitting on the draining board beside the kitchen sink.

"Okay, Mum," replied Shaun. "Thanks. Do you mind if I go upstairs? I've been looking forward to nice hot shower."

"Oh, let me run you a bath," his mum began. She set the dish down with the towel and stubbed her cigarette out in the ashtray, spilling ash onto the table. "You can have a nice long soak with bubbles, the way you used to like it."

Shaun smiled. "Thanks, Mum." She gave him another hug but pulled away again as the tears began to well up. She made her way past Shaun and up the stairs to the bathroom.

Shaun plonked himself down at the kitchen table. He wiped away the spilt ash and emptied the ashtray into the bin behind him.

Maybe everything was going to be okay, he thought. Maybe life *would* get back to normal.

9

DEMON

LONDON'S TRAFFIC PASSED BY MELODY IN A BLURRY HAZE of headlights.

She was sitting on a bench on London's Southbank, waiting for her old colleague and good friend, Reg, to finish work. Boon waited patiently at her feet and seemed to enjoy the noises and smells that accompanied London.

Reg had done well for himself. He'd started his career in tech by hacking into corporations and wreaking havoc, as kids do. But he'd soon developed skills and escalated his antics to larger and more technically challenging hacks. The MoD had been one of those challenges, and subsequently, he'd been caught. His parents had enrolled him in a rehabilitation program for young offenders, and from there, his talents had been spotted, guided, and moulded into a solid tech research operative. His talents had given him experience with the Serious Organised Crime units, from which he'd been asked to join a team of dark ops specialists, who focused on domestic organised crime.

Melody considered his success while she waited for him to finish work in the Secret Intelligence Services building. She pondered on how life had a funny way of working out for some but not for others. It was as if life needed balance. There were choices and then there was balance. If Harvey hadn't joined the team, the cases they'd all worked on together would have had very different outcomes. Perhaps they wouldn't have been so successful.

Maybe some friends that had fallen along the way might still be around. Perhaps Frank, their leader, wouldn't have got so involved. Maybe *he'd* still be alive too.

But the scenes *had* played out, and Melody *had* made the choice to leave the force to live with Harvey in their little French farmhouse, while Reg had been picked up by MI6 and was now an operations team leader, which was led by Jackson, another former team member.

Meanwhile, Melody suddenly found herself very alone with nothing to show for any of her hard work. She'd been told a hundred times that her career possibilities would be endless if she continued on the path she was on. But she'd chosen wrong, and now she was out.

She was out and soon to be married to a man she'd just learned was a serial killer. She laughed to herself, not a hearty laugh, just a disappointed exhale of air that summed up her situation.

She'd known Harvey had been a killer, the whole team had known. That was the very reason he'd been brought into the team. He was the man they had all looked to when there was dirty work to be done. When the regulations and restrictions that bound a government employee prevented them from doing something that was necessary, Harvey was the go-to man. He was unofficially attached to the unofficial dark ops team, and in return, he'd been given a clean slate.

But now, he was muddying the slate he'd worked so hard to clean.

"Penny for them?" a voice said, somewhere far away.

It was Reg. His big childish smile filled his face from ear to ear, as he approached the bench. Melody flung her arms around her old friend. Boon jumped up at them, excited to see Reg. She didn't say hello or ask Reg how he was, Melody just buried her head into his shoulder and held on tightly.

"Hey, what's all this?" he said. He pulled Melody away to take a look at her face, but she kept her head down, embarrassed by her tears.

"Melody, come on, sit down," Reg said gently while making a fuss of Boon.

"I've ruined it," said Melody. "My life. You were right, I *saw* him."

"Melody, come, sit down. Tell me what you saw."

Melody dropped down onto the bench beside him and searched for a tissue in her bag.

"*Blood*, Reg, all over him."

"*Blood?*" asked Reg. "So he-"

"He did it again. The police found a body where we were going to camp, and I saw him. I'd been to town to call you and when I got back, I saw him. I saw him, Reg. *I saw the look*-"

"Whoa, slow down, girl," said Reg. "Where were you?"

"In a village near Chelmsford. Oh God, Reg, what have I done?"

"Let's not be hasty. Let's find out what the police know, and we'll go from there."

"There was a body. It was under a sheet. Red and white tape, uniforms holding back the public, a helicopter. A bloody helicopter, Reg."

He lifted his arm and put it around Melody's shoulders. "Listen to me, Melody, we're going to find a cafe with internet, and we're going to understand what's happening here. Okay?"

Melody was sitting with her head in her hands and didn't respond.

"Melody, right now, you need to be strong. You can get through this. I've seen you pull some seriously crazy stunts, don't let this be the one that breaks you. Come on, let's go." Reg began to walk. "I'm going with or without you, Melody." He shouldered his satchel and began to walk away.

"*Wait*," called Melody.

Reg turned but continued to walk backwards.

"You're right," she said as she straightened. "Wait for me."

George stepped away from the magnetic board and snapped the lid back onto the whiteboard marker.

"There," he said. "Queensbridge, Little Broadwater, King's Lynn, Dunmow and now Rettendon."

"He's moving inland," said Harris, "towards London."

"Not necessarily," said George. "I mean, he might be heading that way, but if he's following the historical murders, he won't go into Central London, he'll skirt around the edge of it. I did a heat map, look." George pulled an A3 printed map of South-East England and stuck it to the board beside the old and new murders.

"It's not hard to see that most of the unsolved crimes on our list, if they were indeed carried out by our man, were all in the East London and Essex areas. He ventured further afield for some, but if he was targeting a particular type of offender-"

"Sex offenders, George. Let's just get it out there," said Harris.

"Right, sex offenders, sir," continued George. "Then he may have been running out of targets and therefore *had* to look further afield."

"George, you're right," said Harris.

"Well, the map doesn't really lie, sir."

"Not the map," said Harris, "but what you said. If he had to look further afield, that means something is driving him to do this. Don't you see?"

"Not really, sir."

"Well, let's make it easy. You like steak, right?"

"Of course, sir, doesn't everyone?"

"But if the supermarket where you did your weekly shopping had run out, you wouldn't bother going to a different supermarket, would you? Not just for steak?"

"No, sir," replied George. "I'd buy something else and hope they had it next week. If they still didn't, I'd re-evaluate where I did my weekly shopping."

"Right," said Harris. "So if the killer was just picking off sex offenders as they cropped up in his neck of the woods, kind of a hatred thing, then all the previous unsolved murders on that heat map would all be in one area. But they're not. Most are, yes, but not *all* of them."

George still didn't understand the analogy.

"Let's put it another way," continued Harris. "If this town ran out of petrol, you would drive to the next one to get it, wouldn't you? Because you *need* petrol, you can't go without it. Whereas you *can* go without steak, it's not a *necessity*."

"I think I understand where you're going with this, sir."

"Something's driving him, George. There's a need, a thirst. He needs to satiate some kind of inner..." Harris searched for the word.

"Demon?" offered George.

"Demon," said Harris excitedly. "If he couldn't find a target when the need came, he *had* to look further afield because he *needed* it, just like you need petrol.

Harris stepped over to the magnetic board, took the

whiteboard marker off George and circled the murders that seemed to be away from the huddle.

"George, my friend," said Harris, standing and throwing the marker back at him, "we have ourselves a demon."

10

WOOD FOR THE TREES

REG AND MELODY WERE SITTING IN A BEER GARDEN outside a pub beside Vauxhall Railway Station. Boon lay under their feet with a small silver bowl that the bartender had kindly provided. Melody had sparkling water and Reg had a pint of diet coke.

Reg flipped open his laptop, connected to his phone's 4G data signal, and flexed his fingers, more for show than anything else.

"Okay," he began, "let's begin with what we know."

"We don't know anything for sure," said Melody. "We know there was another murder, this time in Rettendon. We know that Harvey is involved somehow, and-"

"And that's about all we know, right?" said Reg.

Melody looked slightly dejected but nodded.

"Come on, Melody, we can do this," said Reg. "It's us." He nudged her with his elbow and smiled, giving her a cheeky sideways glance.

"Okay, we also know that more murders happened in the places we've been to," said Melody.

"That-a-girl," replied Reg, happy to see her beginning to

get into the research. "So let's just start plotting a map here. You remember the places?" he asked.

"Queensbridge, Little Broadwater, King's Lynn, and Dunmow. But now we'll need to add Rettendon," said Melody.

"Right," said Reg, "so according to Frank's data, Harvey erm-"

"You can say it, Reg," said Melody. "Harvey murdered somebody in each of those areas."

"Yeah, but it wasn't just murder, was it?" said Reg. "It wasn't a random attack on a member of society."

"No, it was a personal vendetta," said Melody. "For his sister, Hannah, and all the other victims of sex crimes."

"Exactly. According to Frank's files here, Harvey researched these sex offenders and carried out precision killings. Harvey told him that he used to treat them as training."

"That's right. It *was* training," said Melody. "It was how he got so good at what he does."

"Killing?" asked Reg.

"And not getting caught," finished Melody.

"And in the meantime, he found peace for Hannah's memory."

"Yeah, but you know what?" began Melody. "I think there was more to it than that."

"How do you mean?" asked Reg.

"Well, just talking to him about it over the past few days-"

"You talk about all this stuff? Like over breakfast or something?"

"No, not like that. But he's been quiet recently like something has been on his mind."

"You mean the silent, brooding serial killer was quiet over breakfast?"

Melody shot him a look.

"Sorry," said Reg. "Bad taste."

"He's been having dreams," said Melody, "violent dreams, and he gets aggressive in his sleep."

"And what did he say about that?"

"He just said that in the past, he'd had them, and that was like his calling. That was when he'd begin to research a new target."

"So the killing wasn't just to bring peace to Hannah?"

"Yeah, it was," said Melody. "But there's more to it than that. They brought him peace too, kind of like a therapy."

"And he's been having these dreams again?" asked Reg.

Melody nodded. "Yeah, plus he's been quieter and quieter. At first, I thought it was because of the wedding, you know? It's a big deal for him to be centre stage, not hiding in the shadows."

"Okay, can I say something?"

Melody nodded.

"We need to piece this together, but to do it, we're going to need to assume Harvey is guilty, that he's actively killing again, and-"

"I know, Reg," said Melody. "We need to treat him like a suspect and disassociate ourselves from him."

Reg nodded. "Think you can do that?"

"I think I have to," said Melody.

"So we're *not* trying to find him guilty, we're trying to catch him before the police do, and the only way we're going to catch him is by working out where he's going next."

"Reg, no," said Melody. "You could lose your job, aiding and abetting and all sorts."

"If we can get to him, maybe we can get him out of the country, somewhere safe. I don't have to be involved. But you know what? I want to. We owe him that."

"He's already out of control, Reg. I don't know what he's going to do next."

"So where is he now?" asked Reg. "Where did you leave him?"

"Rettendon, by the murder scene," replied Melody.

"Okay, so let's get down and dirty, Melody. Let's see if he has any targets in the area."

"How are you going to do that?"

"The sex-offenders register," said Reg flatly.

"But that won't show their addresses, will it?"

"No, I'd hope not, but I thought you had a little more faith in your old friend than that," said Reg with a smile.

Within a few moments, Reg had an up-to-date copy of the register on his laptop.

"How's this for a hit list?" he said to Melody, showing her the screen.

"There's so many," she said. "These are all-"

"This is all the UK registered sex offenders," said Reg. "Let's start by focusing on Essex and East London."

Reg ran a few commands in the database to add location filters, and the list shrank but still ran off the screen.

"There're still a lot of names there, Reg."

Reg cleared the filters, and the database populated with the full list of names again.

"So, according to Frank's data," said Reg, "I think I'm right in saying that many of the victims-"

"Targets, Reg," corrected Melody.

"Targets?" said Reg.

"That's what Harvey called them, targets. If we're going to find Harvey, we need to think like him."

Reg nodded.

"And besides, Reg, I still love the guy. I don't like to think of him as having victims. He might still be saveable."

"We need to disassociate, Melody," said Reg. "Remember?"

"I am disassociated, Reg. But a girl can cling to hope, can't she?"

Reg gave her a flat smile and carried on.

"Anyway, many of the *targets* were either due to go to trial or had recently been released from prison when Harvey-"

"Killed them," finished Melody. "Killed them violently in the most horrific manner possible, causing slow and agonising deaths." She returned his stare. "I'm okay with it, Reg."

"I'm not sure *I* am," said Reg.

"So who do we have?" asked Melody.

Reg eyed her quizzically.

"Who do we have that's either due up or due out?" said Melody.

"Oh, I see," said Reg, getting back into the research. "Well the database can't actually name people who are yet to be found guilty, for defamation reasons I imagine, but it will show names of people that have recently been released. Let's start with one month, shall we?"

"No, one week," said Melody. "The list will be smaller. Try one week in the London and Greater London areas."

"If you say so," said Reg. His fingers began to fly across the keyboard and the database shrank with each tap of the *enter* key as the filters cleared out the names until they were left with just one.

Shaun Tyson.

Harris was sitting at his desk in his office. The magnetic board displayed a clear picture of the killer's movements over the past couple of weeks and historically. Photos of the victims, locations and methodologies all tied into one and other. But it was all reactive. None of it was a clear indication of what was to come, or where.

That bothered Harris.

Catching a serial killer would propel Harris' career from small-town detective hopefully into something bigger and better. Even if the government agencies got hold of the case and took over, he'd be the one to guide them. He had the research, and he'd been close once before, he'd felt it on that hill. The killer had been close by.

His office door opened, and Malc poked his head into the room.

"Thirsty, Zack?" he asked.

Harris shook his head. "No, Malc, not today, mate. This one needs a clear head."

Malc followed Harris' gaze to the magnetic board and stepped inside to get a better look.

"Oh, for God's sake, Zack," he said. "You could have warned me." He turned away from the ghastly photos of dismembered, burnt, and ruined bodies. "Do you *really* need them up on your wall, Zach?"

"It's good for motivation," said Harris.

"Motivation?"

"He's out there somewhere planning another one, and I'm going to stop him." Harris stared unblinkingly at the wall. He was transfixed.

"Are you sure you're cut out for this?" asked Malc. "Try not to wind up on that wall yourself, eh?"

But Harris was lost in thought.

"Alright, mate, I can see you're busy. Don't be a stranger, eh?"

Harris snapped out of his gaze. "Yeah, sorry, Malc. Got a lot on my plate right now, mate."

Malc peeked behind the door again and studied the mass of sickening photos and George's scribbled writing. "What's all this then?" he asked, pointing at the two lists of old murders and new murders.

"He's done it all before," replied Harris. "We think the killer is re-enacting his previous murders."

Malc's face took on a disgusted look. "He's clearly sick, presuming, of course, it *is* a man?"

"I think so," said Harris. "The last one in Rettendon had a flattened patch of grass beside the body like he'd laid down beside it, maybe even savoured the moment. I had the photographer give me a scale. We're looking for a man, six-foot-ish, average build."

"That narrows it down then," said Malc. But Harris didn't crack a smile.

"I remember this one," said Malc, pointing at a photo of an Eastern European man in what looked like an antique copper bathtub. "Boiled in the bath. I read about that one in the papers."

"Like you said, Malc, he's a sick puppy."

"Yeah but hold on a minute, didn't they find another guy tied up next to the bathtub? It was like the killer had let him go, spared him almost." Malc tapped his forehead trying to think. "Ah, what was his name?"

"Yeah, Shaun Tyson. He's serving time now. George reckons we can't go near him without raising a few unwanted flags, and the last thing I want on this case right now is more attention. It's bad enough that the reporters are hanging around outside, waiting to pounce on me as soon as I step out for a coffee."

"You might want to check that, Zack. This was the guy I was reading about last night. The second guy, Tyson, he's locked up for sex offences, but he's just been released, I'm sure of it. I was round the in-laws last night in Enfield. The guy was from Potters Bar, which is close by, and the local rag did a piece on him. Even had a picture of him at his mum's front door."

"Are you sure it was the same guy?" asked Harris, sitting up from his slouch.

"Yeah, *positive*. The headline was something like 'Boil-in-a-bag Sex Pest Set Free.' You know, imaginative stuff. I doubt he'll make the national papers, but the local one, the Enfield Gazette or something, was having a field day on it. I was surprised they could do that, you know. I mean, the guy is obviously a nonce and needed to be locked up, but the bloke served his time. I said to the missus, when the local boys find out about him, he'll be bloody lynched, he will."

Harris picked up his desk phone and punched a three-digit number.

"George, in here now."

11

DAYS OF THE BEAST

HARVEY STONE WOKE FROM ANOTHER HORRIFIC VIVID dream to find himself under a bridge beside a river. The memory eased slowly into reality and pushed the images of the dead faces from his mind.

He sat upright and clutched his knees to his chest. The cold night had taken hold of his body, and his shirt was damp from the wet ground.

Harvey considered his situation. He was effectively on the run. How had it happened? He'd managed to evade the law his entire life hiding in plain sight, and now he was clean, suddenly he found himself hiding under a bridge. If he was going to make a move, it would need to be now in the early morning light.

He'd watched from the trees as the police had cordoned off the area, and had watched the two plainclothes detectives study the body. He hadn't even had time to study the body himself. He didn't know if the murderer had left clues, but he knew how they'd done it.

Harvey had murdered somebody that way before.

Benjamin Green, Southend-on-Sea. Harvey couldn't

remember when exactly he'd done it, but he knew he had. He'd dreamed of the face. He remembered the sharpened sticks that pinned him to the ground, and the tiny nick of the wind-pipe, not enough to sever it completely, but enough to start the clock ticking. Harvey could see Benjamin in his mind's eye, drowning in his own blood.

The victim on the hill had no face, not in Harvey's memory. In his mind, the face was replaced with a morphed composition of his many targets.

And Melody.

Melody's face. Suddenly it was her lying there on the hill beside him, in his mind. They were rolling around, deep in a passionate embrace, and then blood, thick, hot, sticky blood on Harvey's hands, coming from the back of Melody's head.

He kissed her.

But she wasn't kissing back.

She was lifeless.

He tried to roll her over but she was fixed, her wrists, and her ankles, pinned to the ground by wooden stakes, carved by his own hand.

Her eyes were closed.

He slapped her face.

No response.

"No, Melody," he cried.

He felt her chest.

No movement.

No breath.

"Come on, wake up."

A pool of blood that ran from her sliced throat soaked her mass of thick brown hair as it lay on the sodden ground. Her soft, glowing skin had sunk to a pale white.

Then somebody standing over her.

A shadow.

Harvey lunged out at the shape, but the space was empty.

He fell to the ground and clutched at the small smooth stones beside the river.

Suddenly, he felt as if his chest was being squeezed. He fought for air, but there was none. He rolled back onto his elbows and crawled away from her body, but there was no body, no blood.

Just the shape of a man who standing, unmoving. Watching.

Harvey rolled away in the grass by the side of the bridge and got to his feet. It was daylight now and the river flowed by noisily over the rocks. He peered tentatively under the bridge then all around him.

He felt eyes on him like weights that hung heavy from his limbs.

He found the spot where he'd slept, where he'd seen the body, the faces, Melody's face.

It was a dream; it had to have been. All that lay on the ground now was a makeshift bed of leaves and a crumpled up newspaper he'd used to stop the biting wind.

The newspaper.

Boil-in-the-bag sex pest set free.

"It's here on the right-hand side," said Reg, leaning from the rear of the camper into the front to point at the little house with the wrought iron garden gate and narrow footpath hidden within the quiet back streets of Potters Bar.

Melody drove straight past the house without slowing and found a suitable place to turn the camper around. She parked away from the streetlights, one hundred meters away from the house, turned off the engine and then climbed into the back with Reg, who was pulling the little curtains closed.

"Just like old times, Melody," said Reg, as he passed her a set of binoculars from his pack.

"Except we used to have Harvey *on our side*, Reg," said Melody. "I never thought we'd be *hunting him down*."

"We're not hunting him down, Melody. We're saving the bloke. God knows, *he* saved *us* enough times."

Reg had set up his laptop on the van's small dining table and connected it to his phone's 4G data signal. "You think it's odd that all this is happening at the same time that Shaun Tyson is being let out?" he asked.

Melody lowered the binos.

"Now that you say it, yes."

"But what does that *mean*?" asked Reg. "I mean, who would have known Tyson was being released? And how would Harvey have found out about it?"

"Tons of people would be in the know, Reg," said Melody with a long sigh. "The prison service, family, enemies. Can you imagine how word spreads when somebody like that is set free?"

"Would the media know?" asked Reg.

"I'd hope that they wouldn't, but I guess sometimes information like this is leaked." Melody took a cursory glance through the binos.

"What if it *was* leaked before your trip and Harvey has been leading up to this all along. Planning it. It is, after all, the one guy he spared."

"Oh my God," said Melody. "It was Harvey who suggested stopping in Queensbridge *and* Little Broadwater."

"What about King's Lynn?" asked Reg.

"King's Lynn and Dunmow were my idea, but they were always part of the trip. He knew we'd go to both places. So if he was researching targets, he could have done that weeks ago."

"Here," said Reg, leaning back from his laptop, "there's an

article about Shaun Tyson in the Enfield Gazette yesterday. It says here that-"

"Yesterday?" said Melody. "That can't be it. Check the back issues. If he was planning this all along, he would have had to have known about Shaun a few weeks ago at the very minimum."

"I'm checking the back issues," said Reg. "Doesn't look like anything else has been mentioned about it. So how would he have found out that Tyson was being released?"

Melody gasped. "What about the other targets, the other murders?"

"What about them?" asked Reg.

"When were they released?" said Melody. "If they were already released then maybe Harvey just struck lucky. But-"

"If they had also only just been released, then he definitely has someone on the inside feeding him this information," finished Reg.

"Damn it," said Melody. "I don't know how, but it's somehow worse that all this was premeditated. How could I be so stupid, Reg? He planned this all along."

"Don't beat yourself up about it, Melody. How were you to know?"

"I knew he was a killer, but I thought he was over it. Do you realise how stupid that sounds?"

Reg exhaled through pursed lips. "It doesn't look good, does it?"

Melody held her head in her hands.

"You need to make a choice, Melody."

She looked up and peered through her fingers.

"You need to decide if you're going to help him," said Reg, "or stop him."

Melody stared at Reg with raised eyebrows.

"I love the man, Reg," she said. "But now..." She hung on the words, dreading to say them aloud.

"You have to take him down, Melody," said Reg quietly.

A silence fell between them and Melody's eyes began to glisten in the dark of the camper.

"There's another problem, Reg."

He waited for her to finish.

"He's Harvey Stone," said Melody. "He's unstoppable."

12

CATCHING A DEMON

"ARE WE GOING TO SIT HERE ALL NIGHT?" ASKED GEORGE. "We don't even know if he's going to show up."

"He'll be here alright," replied Harris. "It might be tonight, it could be tomorrow, but he'll be here."

"What makes you so certain?"

"It's all too convenient. Tyson is let out and our man just *happens* to be on a trail of destruction?"

"Yeah, but how would he even know that Tyson has been let out? And even if he did know, he must have known Tyson was being let out-"

"Weeks ago," finished Harris. "The others were just a warm-up."

"A warm up?" said George, incredulous. "You mean like a practice?"

"You saw it yourself, George. The man is good at what he does, but he hasn't struck for a few years. I think he's been honing his skills on whatever scraps he can get and saving himself for this one."

"Tyson?" asked George.

"He's the one guy who got away."

"He let him go though, didn't he?"

"I'm not so sure, George. I mean, why would he let him go?"

"I don't know. This is all just speculation."

"No," said Harris, "we're onto something here. I can feel it. Shaun Tyson was found tied to a wooden beam, while some other guy was boiled to death, right?"

"That's what the reports say," confirmed George.

Harris turned his face away from the headlights of a passing VW camper van that trundled past them.

"The guy that was boiled, what was his name? The Eastern European guy, he was the only one out of all those unsolved murders that wasn't on the sex offenders list, right?"

"Right," said George slowly, trying to see where Harris was going.

"So what if the boiled guy was actually a sex pest, but just hadn't been caught? What if nobody *knew* he was a sex pest apart from our killer? And what if our killer had been looking for this guy all along?"

"I think I'm beginning to see," said George.

"Good, stay with me," said Harris. "So if the killer was hunting the boiled guy all along, it could have taken years, George. Meanwhile, he hunts down known sex offenders, easy targets, to satiate his needs and to hone his skills."

"His demons?" asked George.

"Yeah, you saw the heat map," said Harris. "He stayed local. He only ventured out when the hunger struck and he needed a kill. That's what it is, George. He's got a need, a thirst, and when the need strikes, he kills, but not just anyone, only sex offenders. It's like maybe he was abused or something by the boiled guy? Or maybe someone he was close to was abused, or worse? I don't know. But the boiled guy was the ultimate hit for him, and the killer was angry enough to go vigilante against sex offenders until he found him."

"And that's when the killings stopped," finished George.

"Exactly," continued Harris. "He'd found what he'd been looking for, and his thirst died."

"Only now, his thirst is back," said George.

"And Shaun Tyson is the only man known to have survived this guy."

"So how do you explain the nationwide killing spree in the past two weeks?" asked George.

"Like I said, George, he's reliving the past. He's awakening–"

"The demon?"

"That's right, George," said Harris. His voice lowered, and his eyes focused on the house in front of them. "Tonight, we're going to catch ourselves a demon."

Panic set in the moment Shaun opened his eyes.

His heart raced, and he searched blindly into the dark corners of the room.

He flung back the covers and stepped onto the soft carpet. His confused mind took a few seconds to understand where he was, but then reality caught up, and he leaned with his elbows on his legs and his head in his hands as his breathing calmed and his heart rate slowed.

It would take a while for Shaun to adjust to life on the outside.

No shrieking drug addicts were filling the night, no howling and torturous cries of repent or begging for mercy. There was just silence.

There was no cold brick wall either, or hard concrete floor that welcomed the icy and stale air. There was just the warmth of the central heating and his mother's soft furnishings that retained the heat.

There *was* dark, but Shaun reached for the lamp that was beside his bed, a luxury he'd been without for three years. Nobody could dictate lights off to him anymore. He flicked the light on, off, and back on as if reconfirming the power of choice, a luxury of freedom. He then turned it off once more to enjoy the darkness in safety, the safety of his home, a way of pushing his mind to understand that he no longer needed to live in fear.

Not inside the house anyway.

Shaun rose and walked barefoot to the window. The feeling of the warm, soft carpet under his feet brought a smile to his face. He pulled the curtain back and peered through his bedroom window. He'd had a small window in his cell but the bars had obscured the view and the sloping ledge had prevented him from pulling himself up to see out of it. The most he'd ever seen had been of the dull, grey London sky.

A few houses opposite had lights on, and Shaun felt the urge to wait for a careless neighbour to step out of the shower as he'd done many time before. But he tore his eyes away from the houses, battling to keep his perverse habits at bay.

He focused on the dark instead.

Somewhere out there in the darkness was the girl he'd met in the park that time, the girl that had been so keen to see and feel an adult male in all its glory, yet had run when they had finished and told her mother. He wondered if she was okay. He wasn't sure if it was his own remorse, guilt, or if it was a genuine concern for her he felt, but he certainly felt it. He'd thought about her many times over the past three years. It had started the day after they had met, with lustful images of their short time together, but then, once the police had knocked on his door and taken him away, his thoughts of her had turned to spite and hate. He'd remembered her in the darkness of his single cell, bad thoughts, not the soft touches that he'd remembered fondly, but evil, sadistic thoughts of what he could have done to her. What he should have done.

Maybe?

But the emotions that he felt for her as he was standing by the window in the dark, experiencing his freedom for the first time in three years, were kind. He realised that it hadn't been her fault. He should have known better. No matter how hard she had asked, no matter how relentless her hands had been, he should have walked away.

He hoped she was okay.

He'd considered sending her a note but had been advised that his restraining order would see him back inside. He wondered what might happen if they were to meet on the off-chance on the street, if he would have a chance to tell her how sorry he was. He played the scene out in his mind over and over. The first time around, she was friendly. She'd be older now, maybe even old enough, and they'd held hands. She apologised for what he'd been through, and he told her how he felt, how he'd thought of them together and the softness of her skin. But the scene rolled around again in his mind and returned to them meeting on the street. This time, she screamed for help, shouting that she was being attacked. People recognised him. There were angry men all around, towering above him. But between them, he'd seen her, and she smiled cruelly, a devious evil smile as she watched in the background and the blows had rained down on him from above.

He let his forehead rest against the glass. It was cool and refreshing. It pulled him from his imagination but left the images there as a reminder.

He wondered if he *was* actually better. He wondered if the urges would return. His thoughts suggested they were still there somewhere, hanging in the shadows waiting to strike, waiting for the chance when Shaun's mind was weak, and the opportunity arose.

His mother's disappointed face drifted into his thoughts. She was surrounded by a sea of hate and anger. He remembered that feeling of hatred in everybody's eyes that had stabbed him like daggers as he'd cowered in the dock while the judge and the prosecution had painstakingly carried out the legal procedure to the letter. He'd wished that he could have just told them yes. "Yes, it was me. I did those things. She was innocent, and I took advantage. Now please take me away. Take me away from the eyes, the hate."

It had felt like a lifetime. But when the judge had finally brought his hammer down and declared him guilty on all accounts, and he'd been led shamed from the room, he'd turned briefly to see his mum once more. The look in her eyes had pierced him. While those around her sent sharp, hellish looks of hate, they had merely formed the shaft of the arrow. It had been his mother's disappointed eyes that had formed the sharp point. But not of evil, not of hate, they'd carried a look of shame, a shame so deep and gut-wrenching that he'd been unable to shake it from his mind, even then beside his bedroom window, three years later.

The last image that crossed his mind that evening had been of Pops, of the things he had made Shaun do, and the things he had done to Shaun in return. The old man's rough beard had been abrasive against Shaun's stomach, and his calloused hands around him had been rough, not like hers. He'd tried to contain his arousal at the time, but Pops had been smart, evil but smart. He was always sitting with Shaun and provoking filthy conversations about the dirty things they'd both done. He'd watched as Shaun had relived his time with the girl. Shaun remembered all of the girls, but it was mostly the last girl he fantasised about, the girl who had cried to her mum. Pops had waited to see Shaun's body react, when there was no turning back. Shaun, in his tight tracksuit bottoms, hadn't been able to conceal his arousal and had succumbed to Pop's desires.

Shaun felt sick.

He needed water to wash his mouth of the evil that Pops had put in there. He could feel it. He could taste him.

He began to cry.

But he didn't wail or sob. Prison had taught Shaun to cry quietly. It was best if nobody knew. He wiped the tears from his eyes and reached for the glass of water beside his bed, but movement outside caught his eye. It wasn't much, just a shadow that moved briefly in his mum's back garden. He searched for it again and wiped his eyes with his sleeve to see more clearly. But there was nothing out there except the shed, the greenhouse, and his mum's favourite little apple tree.

13

ABDUCTION

"I HATE SITTING HERE KNOWING THAT HARVEY COULD BE in there right now doing God knows what," said Melody.

"We could move closer?" suggested Reg.

Melody hovered on her answer. "We might drive him away," she said.

"So what's your plan?" asked Reg. "Wait for him to leave and then nab him? We don't even have weapons."

Melody gave Reg a sideways glance.

"You do have weapons, don't you?" he said. "Melody have you been driving around with-"

"I've carried a weapon for nearly ten years, Reg. It's not something I like to leave at home if I can help it. It's a hard habit to break."

Reg shook his head. "I'm seriously going to lose my job, you know that?"

"Who's going to find out?" asked Melody.

"The entire street if you starting opening fire in the middle of the bloody night."

"Relax. I have a suppressor," said Melody. "Besides, we

won't take him down here, we'll follow him. Find somewhere more suitable."

"You're really going to shoot him?"

Melody took a deep breath, and let it out slowly. "I don't see any other option apart from calling it in and watching him be taken away."

"Melody, listen to yourself. You were going to marry this guy and now you're talking about killing him. Maybe we should let-"

"I'm not letting him go to prison, Reg," Melody snapped. "He'd rather be dead than locked up. I know *that* much about him."

"Melody I'm not sure I can be involved," said Reg. "I'm sorry. But I didn't realise we'd be killing anyone, that will just make us as bad as-"

"As bad as him, Reg? No. No, it won't." Melody lifted up the bench seat she had been sitting on and pulled out a long black peli-case.

"Oh no, Melody. I've seen that case before," said Reg.

Melody popped open the two latches and lifted the lid.

"Oh for God's sake," said Reg. "When you said you were carrying, I thought you meant a little Sig handgun or something, Melody."

Melody began to build her Diemaco sniper rifle. She kept her head down and continued to piece the gun together as she spoke.

"Have you ever fired a handgun, Reg?" she asked, as she snapped the stock into place.

"In training, and once or twice in-"

"Did you ever *hit* anything, Reg?" she asked.

"Well, come to think of it, no. No, I didn't."

"Do you know how close you'd need to be to take someone down with a handgun, Reg?" She stopped what she was doing and looked up at her friend.

"Erm, well no," he replied.

"You *could* get lucky. You could hit him in the head. But even from twenty metres away, the odds are against you."

She started to load the magazine with rounds from a brand new box.

"So imagine this," she continued, "you're twenty metres away from someone, a trained man, quick and agile, and you miss your first head shot. Close your eyes and imagine it, Reg. Tell me what happens next. Tell me how it plays out."

Reg took a breath and closed his eyes.

"Erm, I take another shot?"

"Did you even aim? Are you nervous?"

"Yeah, I'm aiming."

"At his head? He's turned. He sees you."

"Yeah."

"He's coming for you, fifteen steps."

"I fire again."

"That's still a tough shot, Reg. You missed. You're shaking with adrenaline and fear."

"I'd go for the body; it's a bigger target."

"Five steps away."

"Even I couldn't miss from there."

"Bang. Too late. He's on top of you. He's wounded, he might even be dying, but he's disarmed you and just put the gun to your head."

Reg was silent for a moment. "It happens that quick?" he asked.

"Now," said Melody, as she snapped the magazine into the rifle's slot, stood the gun upright on its butt, and closed the lid of the case, "imagine it's Harvey you were firing at."

It was a strange feeling for Shaun, as he sat at his mum's

kitchen table in the dead of night. His head was thick with the pressure that formed from a whirlwind of emotions, guilt and mostly shame, but also the desire not to be a bad person, not to go back to prison, and not to let shame rain down on his mum. She deserved better.

It was with these words that Shaun finished his note and scrawled his name with an X underneath it.

He told her he loved her and would be back once his head was clear. He hoped she'd understand, and he would, of course, phone, so she would know how he was doing and where he was.

Shaun didn't fold the note. He left it on the table by the ashtray where she would see it as soon as she woke up.

The trip away would do him good. It might even toughen him up a little and teach him to stand on his own two feet. He'd heard a guy in prison talk about how he went travelling when he was younger, and Shaun had marvelled at his courage. At just eighteen, Jason King had jumped on a ferry with barely enough money to get to him through a few weeks of eating poorly and sleeping in hostels or on a beach. But he'd done it and survived with so many wonderful tales.

"Life has a funny way of working out," Shaun remembered him saying.

Shaun recalled how Jason had found buses and trains to get him to the coast, then either walked for miles or scrounged rides where he could to get to the next town or village. He'd ended up joining a few other travellers and picked fruit for a small wage and free board in an old shack. Then, when the season was up and he'd saved enough money for the next stage of his journey, Jason had moved onto another adventure.

Prison life had allowed time for Shaun to think. Often his thoughts felt like they were hideous B-movies that had been cast by the devil himself. But sometimes, a positive thought slipped through and found its way to the front of his mind. Life on the outside, a new beginning, a fresh start. Whichever form they came in, they encouraged the hope that had been suppressed by the evil inside him.

It was hope that now ran freely in his thoughts.

Thoughts of what France might look like, or what it might be like to once more stand amongst peers, and not be *that* guy, to not be avoided. Most of all, Shaun clung to the hope of one day being normal.

He could have listened to Jason talk all day about how beautiful Austria is and what life is like in Amsterdam cafes, about Roman architecture and the treasures to be found in the small villages that dot Europe's countryside. But Jason's audience had been a party of imprisoned perverts who, each time Jason had begun an anecdote, had steered the tales of wonder onto the less pleasant topic of sex and debauchery.

Shaun had quietly considered Jason's stories of the girls that he'd met on his travels, and he'd felt a pang of jealousy at how easily Jason had spoken to them. Jason had said that people are more comfortable approaching a man on his own, whereas they might hesitate before talking to a group of guys. Shaun would like that. For someone to ask if he'd like to join them doing whatever they were doing, dinner, drinks, or even just laying on a beach chatting.

Shaun had a plan, albeit rough and loose. He'd walk through the night, just to get away from Potters Bar; that was the first and most crucial part of his escape. If he tried to leave during the day, his mum would hold him back with her emotional ties.

Then the devil inside would smile at his captivity, and creep out from the shadows again. He needed to strike while hope ran freely through his mind.

In the morning, he'd be far away enough to find a train or a bus station, where he'd start his journey south to Dover and wait for the ferry to France. It might take him a day to get there, he didn't even know how far Dover was from Potters Bar, but it didn't matter. He'd get there eventually. There was no time constraint, and freedom truly did lie outside the door.

All he needed to do was strike up the courage to take the first step.

He'd emptied his little savings pot that he had in his bedroom, and then shamefully taken the envelope that his mum kept in an old coffee pot in the kitchen. He knew she would be angry, and he'd tell her as soon as he could, once he was far away. She'd understand. It was all to make him better.

He got to his feet and collected his little rucksack from the floor. He hadn't taken much, just a few changes of clothes, his trainers, his passport and the photo of his mum that he'd kept in his prison cell.

Shaun gave the room a final glance and made sure the note was in full view. Then he turned out the light and closed the kitchen door quietly.

A nervous smile crept onto his face when he opened the front door and stared out at the dark and empty street. Freedom is just a few steps away, he told himself. He zipped up his jacket, stepped out into the night, and closed his mum's front door behind him.

Shaun noticed that since he had begun to prepare for the trip, which had been just an hour, he'd managed to restrain his evil thoughts more easily, and more positivity was being let through.

Things were changing.

Life has a way of working out.

He took a final look up at the house and thought to himself that he'd return a few months or a year from now. Maybe he'd have a girlfriend. Maybe he'd find success as well as growth on his travels. But whatever happened, when he returned, he would be a changed man, of that Shaun was sure.

That was the last positive thought he had that evening.

A strong hand reached from behind him and forced a chloroform-soaked rag to his open mouth.

Shaun struggled, he even kicked out at his assailant, but within a few seconds, his knees buckled and he fell limply to the ground.

14

CHOICES

"Whoa, Melody, we have action," said Reg.

Melody jumped up and reached for her binoculars. She saw the limp, unconscious body of Shaun Tyson being dragged into the side door of a black van.

"I see him," she said. "I knew it, Reg."

"Are you going to take him out?" asked Reg.

"No, not here, there'd be too many eyes. Let's tail him and see where he takes him."

Reg loitered, half standing and half crouching in the back of the camper.

"You drive, Reg," said Melody.

"I knew you were going to say that," replied Reg, grumbling as he climbed into the driver's seat. He started the camper's engine but kept the headlights turned off.

"Keep the lights off," said Melody from the back.

"Yeah, I remember," said Reg. "This ain't my first rodeo you know?"

The black van pulled away slowly and its headlights flicked on a few moments later when halfway down the street.

"This ain't his first rodeo either," said Reg quietly. He engaged first gear and pulled out into the quiet road.

The VW camper rode the tarmac smoothly, and Reg waited for the black van to turn out of the street before he gunned the throttle to reach the end of the road, where he saw the van disappear around a bend.

"Keep this distance," said Melody.

"Is it safe to turn the lights on now?" asked Reg.

"I thought you said this weren't your first rodeo?"

"Well, you know," replied Reg, "I don't want to upset my Jedi master."

Melody didn't smile at the joke. She was focused on the van in front.

Reg clicked the light switch on the dashboard and the headlights flicked on. He followed the black van in front, as it weaved through the maze of backstreets and onto Potters Bar high street.

"He's heading for the motorway," said Melody, seeing the van turn left.

"We can't take him out there," said Reg.

"No, but if he's going where I think he's going, we'll have our chance."

"I can't believe we're actually doing this," said Reg.

"What?" said Melody. "Saving lives?"

"Going after Harvey. He's still one of us."

Melody sat forward.

"That's how I was thinking, Reg," she replied. "But you have to remember that Harvey won't be thinking like that. He's ill, he must be."

"Like mentally?"

"How else would you explain it? You see what he's done, you know what he's been through. It would have broken most men, but Harvey pulled through. On the exterior, he's this tough, no-nonsense guy that's afraid of nothing."

"But on the inside?" asked Reg.

"On the inside, Reg, he's hurting. He knows it's not normal to do this. He knows *he's* not normal. I often wondered if he yearns for normality, or if he even knows what normality *is*."

"You don't think it's some kind of destiny?" asked Reg.

"I doubt he believes it's destiny. In Harvey's mind, things just are, or they're not. Things happen, or they don't. You plan for them, or you don't. You live-"

"Or you die," finished Reg.

"Exactly."

"We're approaching the motorway, Melody."

"Keep your cool and stay well back. The motorway is well lit and he'll spot the camper a mile away."

"Do you think he'll spot that BMW?"

"What BMW?" asked Melody.

"The one that's been following us all the way from Potters Bar."

"You're getting restless, George," said Harris. "Can you try and keep still? The way the car is bouncing around people will think we're up to no good in the back seat."

"I can't help it, sir," replied George. "I need to stretch my legs."

"What are you, a kid? Calm down. We're onto something good here. Just think of the glory, George."

"Glory?" said George. "Do you honestly think he's going to turn up just because-"

"He'll be here, George," interrupted Harris.

"I know, you can feel it your bones, right?" said George. "I just wish I could feel a nice pint of lager in my hand instead of cramp in my legs. Sod the bloody glory."

Harris gave him a sharp look.

"I asked you if you were up for this, George."

"I *am* up for it, sir," replied George. "It's just bloody boring is all. It would help if we could actually see the front of the house. All I can see is that van-"

"Which makes this a perfect position, George. We see everyone who comes and goes, and they don't see us."

"I'm bringing a book next time."

Harris looked across slowly with a frustrated look on his face.

"Here I am, trying to bring you on, help you climb the ladder, George, and yet all I hear is you moaning about cramp and boredom."

"I can't help it, sir."

"Think about that board in my office, George," said Harris. "Think about the faces of those men in the pictures."

"You mean the dead sex-offenders, sir?"

"I mean the faces of human beings, George," said Harris. "There's a man out there with a taste for blood. He's outwitted the police for twenty years. He cuts people to ribbons, burns and boils them alive. He's a twisted man. It doesn't matter if he's a vigilante trying to do good, to me, he's a killer, a madman. He's loose, he's dangerous, and he won't stop until someone stops him."

"And that someone is-"

"That someone is me, George." Harris spat as he said the words. He'd wound himself up. "We're going to take him down, and you can either carry on moaning about cramp and boredom, or you can help me catch him, and just maybe you'll learn enough to get a foot on that ladder."

George listened to his superior's rant with real affection for his positivity.

"You honestly think we can do this?" he asked.

"Yes, George," said Harris. "I honestly think that when,

not if, but *when* our man comes walking down this street and gets into that house over there, we'll be on top of him."

A vehicle started its engine somewhere in the quiet street.

"What's that?" asked Harris, turning and looking through the rear window. "Look alive, George. Where's that engine coming from?"

"It's the van, sir," said Harris excitedly. "It's on the move."

Harris spun back to face the front and watched as the large black van pulled slowly from its parked position on the side of the road and began to make its way up the street.

"Aren't we following, sir?" asked George.

"All in good time, Georgy," said Harris. He stared transfixed at the van. "All in good time, my friend."

Harris' hand moved to turn on the car's ignition.

"Hold on, sir," began George. "Look behind, there's another van pulling out."

"That's a camper van," said Harris. "That would explain how he gets about, but who's in the black van then?"

"You think he has help?" asked George.

Harris' eyes widened.

"We never even thought of that," he replied.

"What do we do?" asked George, suddenly sounding nervous.

Harris let the van pass, waited a few seconds, and then started the BMW.

"We let it play, George."

"But there'll be more than one of them."

"And there's more than one of us. What's the problem?"

"Well, what if there's three of them?"

"Then we call in backup, George," said Harris, as he edged the car away from the kerb. "This is a real find. If we need help, we'll ask for it. But if we can handle it, then we'll handle it."

"Righto, sir," said George, sounding unsure.

"Do you feel it George?" asked Harris.

"Feel what, sir?"

"The electricity. Can't you feel it thundering through you?"

"Not really, sir," said George. "But my cramp's going away."

"Well, you might want to forget about your cramp, George, and start to tune yourself into this."

George stared at the van in front and saw the lights turn on once it was away from the house.

"Have you ever done this kind of thing before, sir?"

"Have I ever captured a serial killer, sorry, serial *killers*?" said Harris. "No, George, as it happens, no, I haven't. But you know what? All that is about to change."

"Looks like he's joining the motorway, sir," said George.

"Where's he taking us?" said Harris under his breath.

He reached under his seat and fumbled around, then brought out a small Glock handgun. He hit the little silver button on the left side of the moulded grip and let the magazine fall into his lap.

"There's a box in the glove compartment," he said, handing the empty magazine to George. "Load that."

"A gun?" said George. His voice rose a full tone. "Where the bloody hell-"

"George, load the bloody weapon and stop acting like a kid."

"But, sir, we aren't supposed to-"

"We aren't supposed to do a lot of things, George," snapped Harris. "But we do, don't we? Because it gets the job done, doesn't it? And right now, Georgy, we have two targets, both of which are prime suspects in a serial homicide investigation."

"Two suspects," said George, suddenly grasping something. "The camper, sir. It's the same one."

"Same one as what?"

"Rettendon, sir," said George. "I thought it looked familiar. It was at the crime scene. The uniform was questioning the driver, a girl with a dog. Remember?"

"George, you clever bastard," said Harris. "You're right. That, my friend, is far too much of a coincidence for my liking."

"It's turning off the motorway, sir."

"Where's she going then? Think fast, George."

"Okay, what if the van is an innocent and the killer is in the camper? Maybe Shaun Tyson got in the van without us seeing, and maybe the camper was waiting for him to pull away."

"Or, what if there really are two killers and one's leading us on a little magical mystery tour?"

"Gut feeling, sir?" asked George as he loaded the magazine with the brass rounds from the little cardboard box in the glove compartment.

The atmosphere in the car had grown thick as the drama unfolded, and the decision time had come from out of nowhere.

"Gut feeling, it's the camper van," said Harris. "Are you sure it's the same one?"

"I'm positive, sir," said George. "But I'm sure I can see someone in the back window."

"So how about this?" said Harris. "There's two of them. It's a couple-"

"Like Bonnie and Clyde?"

"They'd blend in everywhere," said Harris.

"And who'd suspect a woman of being capable of doing those things?"

Harris began to pull off the motorway, following the camper at a safe distance. They both watched as the black van continued on its path and then was out of sight.

"I hope you're sure about this, sir," said George.

15

OLD TIMES

"I HOPE YOU'RE SURE ABOUT THIS, MELODY," said REG, as he pulled the camper off the motorway onto the slip road and watched the black van drive away.

Melody took a deep breath and exhaled through pursed lips.

"Only one way to find out, Reg," she said.

The slip road led down to a roundabout, where the right-hand exit led under the motorway and into London, and the left-hand exit led into Epping Forest and the countryside beyond.

"They're following," said Melody, gazing out the rear window.

"Which way?" asked Reg. "Left or right?"

Melody took a few seconds to look at the options.

"Left," she said. "We need to find a quiet road in the forest."

"What are you planning, Melody?"

"Something Harvey showed me once," she said. "It somehow seems apt right about now."

"Who are they?" asked Reg. "Why do you think they're following us?"

"Police," said Melody flatly. "I'm sure I saw that car in Rettendon with two men in the front."

"That particular car?"

"That particular car, Reg. They were detectives, plain clothes, and if they did their homework just like we did ours, then they must have come to the same conclusion, and knew Harvey was going to strike as soon as Shaun Tyson was released."

"So why's he following us?" asked Reg. "We're not the bloody killer."

"No, but *they* don't know that," said Melody.

"If they think it's us then we need to either lose them or finish this soon," said Reg. "They could have back up ready to block the roads. All they'd have to do is call it in."

"I don't think we're going to lose them in this camper van, Reg," said Melody, as she armed the rifle. "We're going to have to do this the hard way."

"Just hold on a minute, Melody," said Reg, turning in his seat. "You might be bleeding bonkers enough to shoot a policeman. But you know what? I'm not. I don't want to lose my job. I suddenly don't want any part of this. It's going from bad to worse."

"I thought you were talking earlier about Harvey being one of us?"

"I did, I was, he is, or was," said Reg in a panic. "But there's no way I'm being involved in shooting policemen, or anybody, come to think of it. You've gone nuts, Melody. You've spent far too much time with Harvey."

"And what's that supposed to mean?" snapped Melody. "Too much time? I love the man. Of course I spent time with him."

"And he's rubbed off on you. There's no way you would even consider shooting a policeman a year ago."

"Reg, just calm down and keep your eyes on the road," said Melody calmly. "Whatever happens, we're not going to let these detectives take Harvey down. If he's going to be stopped, it's going to be me that stops him, not someone who doesn't understand him. He won't deal with that well."

"So...?"

"So I want you to gently slow down, just a fraction, Reg, and I'm going to count down from three. When I say the number one, I want you to brake hard."

Melody crept beneath the rear window and loosened the locks on either side of the clear Perspex. She took a glance and placed the BMW at five hundred yards back.

"Slower, Reg. We need them closer."

"You're crazy, Melody," replied Reg. "I don't like this at all."

"Reg, do you trust me?"

Reg hesitated.

"Reg, I asked if-"

"Of course I trust you. I think you've gone nuts but I trust you. I'm still driving, aren't I?"

"That-a-boy, Reg," she replied quietly. "Now slow down a bit more, just ease off the accelerator a little."

The camper began to slow, just enough to allow the BMW to slowly close the distance.

"Okay, that's good," said Melody. "Now I want you to indicate left as if you're going to pull over."

Reg did as he was instructed, and the BMW grew closer still. Melody watched with a trained eye. She tried to think like the detectives. She had been one for so long, so it came naturally.

"They're going to pretend to pass slowly, and then cut us off. Are you ready for the hard brakes?"

Reg shook his head in disbelief. "Yes, Melody," he said. "I'm ready, but this is on you."

"Three."

Reg took a deep breath.

"Two. Easy now, Reg."

"I'm easy," he said, unable to hide his nerves.

"One."

———

Panic set in the moment the van took a corner at speed, sending Shaun sliding across the wooden floor into the side panel, waking him from his drug-induced sleep. The bag over his head was rough on his face, like Pop's beard had been, and his wrists were bound with what felt like gaffer tape.

Shaun struggled to control his breathing, trying in vain to see through the bag's material. But the van was dark and offered no indication of size, or even if he was alone.

"Is anyone there?" he whispered.

No reply.

"Hello?" he said, slightly louder.

The rumble of the road noise and the van's diesel engine were the only replies.

He worked his way into a corner by sliding like a worm, and then pushed with his bare feet against the wooden floor and his face against the metal side of the van until he was sitting upright.

Then the tears came again.

Shaun thought of his mum. She wouldn't even know he was in trouble. She would find the note, she'd be upset, but Shaun had hoped she'd be happy that he was off on a quest to better himself, to be a better person, and to finally make a go of life.

Except he wasn't. His quest had ended after just one step.

There would be no trip to Europe. No hitch-hiking, no fruit picking, no sleeping rough, no making friends, no meeting girls.

It wasn't the first time Shaun had been tied up and thrown into the back of a van, but he sensed it would be the last. The brutality of the attack flashed across his mind. Strong, practised hands had held him and forced the chemical-soaked cloth onto his mouth and over his nose. He'd tried to move his head away, to gasp at fresh air, but he'd been easily overpowered.

His nose ran, but all he could do was reach up with his shoulder and smear snot across his wretched face inside the bag.

He was helpless.

"Is anybody there?" he called out again, slightly louder than before. But again, no replies were offered. Just the rumble of the road and hum of the van.

The noise was constant. He gauged the speed at motorway speed. He hadn't felt a turn for a while.

Shaun was tired. Emotionally exhausted. The joy of being released from prison after three years had been tainted by the ever-present shame and guilt that had coursed through him as a reminder that he was a sick and twisted man. Then the feeling of control he'd felt in the kitchen had been wonderful, almost uplifting. He was leaving, he was heading off to Europe to better himself, to make his mum proud of him again, and now fear had returned and sunk its bitter teeth into his skin.

He'd taken one step and been cut down.

He began to shiver, from both the fear and cold, so much so that his torso began to ache. With his legs pulled up to his chest, he forced his bound wrists over his knees to hold himself and preserve any body heat he could. In doing so, he felt the gaffer tape stretch, just a little.

But it was enough to spark hope.

Maybe he could escape? Maybe he still had a chance? His bag. Shaun remembered he had a multi-tool in the top pocket. It had been a gift from his mum and he'd never used it.

He felt around with his feet for the bag's soft material. Had he dropped it? Had his assailant taken it? Was it on the seat in the front beside him as he drove?

His foot touched something soft.

It felt like his bag.

Shaun pushed himself flat on the floor and shuffled across to it. Elation set in followed closely by desire.

He found the multi-tool.

From memory, he knew that the fold-out blade was on one side with a little groove for his thumbnail to pull at. He fumbled with it and finally felt the blade release stiffly from its folded position.

A few awkward moments later, the tool was in his hand with the blade turned inwards, and he began to cut the tape.

The van slowed and took a long sweeping bend. Shaun steadied himself. His heart began to race. Hope was winning the race of emotions in his mind, but the van's movements meant the driver might be close to where wherever it was they were heading.

He didn't have long.

His breath felt hot and sour in the bag, and his breathing quickened, multiplying the heat and the foulness of his own adrenaline-fueled breath. The angle he was cutting at made applying pressure on the blade difficult, but he developed a slow rhythm and felt like he was making progress.

The van turned again, this time the opposite way, sending Shaun rolling onto his front. He outstretched his arms and took the brunt of the landing on his elbows. The blade was perilously close to his neck.

In an instant, his mind flashed with old memories of suicide. Dreams he'd had. The things he'd considered.

Death took a step forward.

Shaun pushed himself to his knees.

But not yet.

He resumed cutting at the tape with added vigour. Soon, he felt the blade break through the final strand of his restraints, and he pulled his wrists apart feeling the cool air on his skin. He set the multi-tool down and immediately tore the remains of tape away then frantically began to pull at the bag on his head.

It was tied at the back of his neck.

His breathing quickened once more, and he was thrown off balance as the van turned, more sharply this time. It began to slow.

He couldn't figure out the knot. He couldn't find the loose end to pull.

The van slowed further and felt like it had turned into a driveway as the tyres found noisy gravel, and the slow crunching of stones began.

Shaun fumbled for the tool. He couldn't lose *that*. He cut a hole by his mouth and sucked in the cool air then cut the bag across his face and pulled it over his head as if removing a hood.

The back of the van was pitch dark, and his eyes adjusted merely to the new shade of black.

The sound of gravel had finished, but the van continued to roll forward over bumpy ground. There was a small incline then the sound of a wheel driving over a stick.

He tried to picture the scene for his escape.

The back of the van had two doors, the side and the rear. He edged closer to the back doors and fumbled for the door release. Perhaps he could run. The van was moving slowly enough; he could easily jump out. He could be gone before the driver knew.

The door was locked.

Which door would the driver open? The side door was on the opposite side of the driver seat. So maybe he'd just walk to the back and open the rear door? But maybe he'd walk around the front of the van and open the side door?

The van stopped.

Shaun crouched, ready to pounce.

The engine turned off.

Shaun listened but heard only the sound of his own breathing and the regular beating of his heart.

The driver opened the door and slammed it closed.

Shaun was half standing, poised between the two doors, and holding the blade ready to slash out at whoever opened the van.

He heard footsteps outside. But from which direction?

A stream of saliva leaked from his mouth like a salivating animal.

This was survival.

But no door opened.

The footsteps disappeared.

Shaun trembled in the darkness for what seemed like an eternity.

Then, out of nowhere, he heard the rush of petrol being ignited.

16

DARK REALITY

HARRIS SLOWED THE CAR AS THE CAMPER IN FRONT EASED to the side of the road. Its brake lights cast hues of red onto the underside of the canopy of trees, formed by the forest that reached across the road as if it were somehow trying to reclaim the space.

"Easy now, George," said Harris quietly. "I'll stay in the car, and you talk to the driver. Get him out of the vehicle."

"But what if-"

"I'll be covering you from here. Nothing's going to happen," said Harris, as he racked a round into the handgun.

"This isn't turning out to be a fun night for me, is it?" said George, as he reached for the door handle.

The interior light flashed on brightly, and Harris squinted through the windscreen to keep an eye on the camper.

George climbed out of the car, closed the door and the interior light slowly dimmed, returning Harris to darkness. He watched as George took a wide path around to the driver's door, then saw him ask the driver to step out.

Suddenly, the rear window sprang open and the muzzle of a high calibre rifle shot out. Within moments, it had fired a round, and Harris felt the car drop as the front left tyre burst. Before Harris could react, the rifle aimed at him.

The camper began to indicate then pulled out onto the road again and drove away casually.

"Shit, shit, shit," said Harris. He thumped his hand on the steering wheel and tossed the handgun into the back of the car.

George had dropped to the ground when he heard the gunshot and now sat up in the middle of the road looking confused. Harris climbed out and surveyed the damage.

"What the hell just happened there?" said George.

"Did you get a good look at the driver?" asked Harris.

"Male, IC1. Small frame, gaunt face, glasses, messy brown hair, I think. He looked almost nerdy. Who took the shot?"

"There was a woman in the back of the camper," replied Harris.

"The one from Rettendon?"

"Can't be sure, George," said Harris. "I was concentrating on the rifle she aimed at me."

"*She aimed at you?* Shall we get uniforms to stop them? They can't get too far."

Harris thought about it. "No, wait," he said. "They're going somewhere local. Get that wheel changed. They won't be going far."

George dropped his arms to his sides and shook his head, then walked to the back of the car to get the tools and the spare wheel. Harris joined, and took the jack from him.

"Do you know where we are, George?" asked Harris.

"Yeah, this is Waltham Abbey," said George.

"No, I mean, do you know *where* we are?"

George looked puzzled. "*Waltham Abbey*, sir," he replied. "Essex?"

Harris had found the car's jacking point and was winding the jack handle to lift the vehicle. "What's that way?" he asked, nodding west, back towards the direction they had come.

"London, sir," replied George.

"In particular, what part of London?"

"East London I guess, sir."

Harris stopped winding and looked up at George, who was pulling the spare wheel from the boot.

"Okay, I'll spell it out for you, George," said Harris. "We're in Essex. East London is a spit away. But not only are we in Essex, we're literally *inside* Epping Forest." He motioned at the trees around them.

George's eyes widened. "The murders, sir."

"The magnetic board in my office, George," continued Harris. "Think about it. That camper didn't just turn around and go back to the motorway, did it?"

"No, sir."

"They headed that way, and the black van on the motorway, George, it wasn't in the fast lane, was it?"

"No, sir, it was in the slow lane, as if it was going to take the next exit," said George, suddenly seeing where Harris was going.

"We're close, George."

"But where?" asked George. "I mean, it's a big old place, Essex."

"All the murders so far have taken place in the victim's homes, or somewhere quiet like a forest, right?"

"Right. Apart from Rettendon, that one was out in the open," said George.

Harris cracked the last wheel nut with the tyre brace and began to spin the tool in his hands. "But," he said, as he removed the last nut, "it was *still* a quiet place, beside a forest."

"Yeah," said George, "and there's no saying he didn't do

the killing *in* the forest and carry the body to where we found him."

"Right," said Harris. "Your man, the driver, was he short?"

"Short, sir?" said George, as he took the damaged wheel off Harris and rolled the new one to him.

"In height, George, was he tall or short?"

"Short, sir," replied George. "Well, not tall anyway."

"And slight, you say. He was small framed?"

"Yes, looked like he'd break if the wind blew too hard, sir."

"Did he look like the man who flattened the grass beside the Rettendon murder?"

George pictured the image in his head for a moment. "No, sir, but-"

"That means there's a few of them in on this," said Harris, as he spun the wheel brace and secured the spare tyre in place. He heaved himself up, tossed the brace to the floor and wiped his hands on a cloth that George offered.

"They're covering for each other. They're covering each other's tracks. They're creating alibis. It's not one man doing this, it's a bloody team, George."

"You think the bigger man was in the back van?"

"That's exactly what I think," said Harris, nodding for George to pick up the old tyre and put it in the boot.

"But we don't know where, sir. We still don't know where they're going to be."

"They like seclusion, George. They like to take their time. They're re-enacting the killings, perfecting them, every detail improved."

"Every detail, sir?"

"Every detail," said Harris. "The photos, George. The stakes that he carved to pin his victim to the ground."

"What about them?"

"Think of the photos of the first time. The stakes were

handmade, but they were amateur. The second time around, George, the stakes were perfectly smooth, as if someone had taken the time to-"

"I'm with you," said George. "He wanted to make it better than before."

"He wanted it perfect, George."

"And Noah Finn," continued Harris, "the first time he did it, the body had been laying there for so long that nobody could even tell what had happened until it was examined."

"But this time he made sure we would find it straight away."

Harris' mind wandered and pictured the image of the boiled man, where Shaun Tyson had been found.

"The boiled man, the last of the old murders," he said.

"What about him?" asked George.

"Where was he found? Where was Tyson found?"

"I think it was in the basement of some big house."

"Can you be more specific?"

George opened the car door and reached for his notes and files. He flicked through until he found the printout.

"Theydon Bois, sir."

"The boiled man, George, that's the next death. And what better place to re-enact the scene than the original location? The place where Shaun Tyson was spared the first time around."

"They're going to boil him," said George.

Harris slammed the boot of the car.

"Not if we can help it, George."

"Go, go, go, Reg," shouted Melody, as soon as she saw the tyre explode.

She aimed at the driver as a warning not to try to follow

them. Once they were far enough away, she collected the spent round that was ejected from the rifle and ducked below the camper's rear window in case return shots were fired.

"How's that right foot of yours, Reg?" she asked.

"Erm, fine," replied Reg, turning to see her making her way up the aisle.

"Well stick it to the floor," she said. "We've got a murder to stop."

"And where exactly is it we're going? We lost Harvey, remember?"

"There's only one place he *can* go," she said thoughtfully. She glanced across at Reg's face and saw his expression turn to dismay.

"Not?"

"The same place he took Shaun before, Reg," said Melody. "It's the only place he'll get the privacy he needs. The place is special to him somehow."

"He needs privacy?" asked Reg.

"And time."

"To prepare?" asked Reg.

Melody gave him a look.

"He's going to boil him, isn't he?" said Reg.

"Not if we can stop him, Reg."

"What happens if they call it in?"

"Who? The boys in blue back there?" asked Melody. "They won't be calling anything in. The force is full of wanna-be heroes like that. They stumble onto something like this and see the potential glory. Greed and a step up the ladder are far too attractive for them to consider sharing the reward with a bunch of uniformed police."

"Ordinarily I'd agree, Melody," said Reg. "But we're not talking about stopping a mugging or a car theft. This is Harvey Stone we're talking about."

"They don't know that, Reg, do they?" she replied. "As far

as they're concerned they're onto a madman on a killing spree. What could be better than bringing him in single-handed and nailing him for the recent murders, *and* dragging up the past with all the historical stuff?"

"But Frank wiped his slate clean. They can't nail him for those now, surely?"

"Either way, Reg, it's not going to be a fun time for Harvey. He's already looking at five life sentences back to back, six if we don't get there in time."

Reg was silent for a while, and Melody stared out of the window at the passing trees.

"Thanks, Reg," she said.

"Thanks for what?" he replied.

"For staying and helping. For being a friend. I'm not sure I could do this alone."

Reg forced a smile. "You have a plan yet?"

"I need to talk to him," said Melody. "I need to get to him before he finishes Shaun Tyson. If he kills Shaun, he'll be gone again, and that'll be the last I see of him."

"Maybe that's for the best, Melody," said Reg. "Maybe letting him finish what he started will really be the end of all this."

"I'd love to believe that." Melody held back the tears. "But I got so close to him Reg. He was normal; or rather, I thought he was. Things were great. I just didn't see this coming. Sure, I knew about his past, but we all did, right? We saw the change in him. We saw the good in him. I just can't believe that this evil was suppressed inside him for all this time."

"Are you sure you even *want* to see him again?" asked Reg. "I mean, knowing what you know now."

"I'm one of the few people he won't kill, Reg," said Melody. "I owe it to myself to close this off before he either goes missing or is killed himself."

"You think he'll die for this?"

"He won't go to prison, Reg. I think we both know that much."

"Yeah but he wouldn't-"

"Kill himself?" finished Melody. "No, he'd never do that. But he'd die fighting." She turned away and wiped a small tear that had formed in the corner of her eye. "Of that I'm certain."

17

THE EYES OF THE BEAST

ONLY THE CRACKLE OF A NEARBY FIRE COULD BE HEARD outside the van. Shaun remained poised to jump out of whichever door opened first.

His ears were now attuned to the sounds around himself and the van. The darkness had dulled his vision and heightened his audible sensitivity, the crack of a branch or snapping of a stick, the sounds of something heavy being dragged across the rough ground.

A man panting from exertion.

Shaun tried to remember what the other man had looked like, all those years ago. He remembered the night well, seeing a man boiled alive and knowing that he was next in line had left an indelible mark on Shaun's memory. He remembered the eyes most of all.

The eyes of the beast.

They had been cold eyes, hard and emotionless, and given the chance, Shaun could probably draw them. They were like no other eyes he'd ever seen.

A vision of the beast that had tied him to the wooden beam and forced him and the other man to reveal their dirty secrets ran across Shaun's mind. Death had hung in the air and seemed to take a step closer with every word Shaun had said during his confession. He'd tried to prolong the story, to keep death at bay, but the story had eventually ended.

Shaun had then been forced to listen with horror as the man who lay beside him had recounted a night long ago when he'd raped the beast's sister. It hadn't been just him, there'd been others. But he'd confessed, and he'd paid the price.

Shaun saw the man in his mind's eye, dragging wood to the fire outside, preparing Shaun's death.

Harvey. That had been his name, thought Shaun. He hadn't thought of the name for a long time, and now it came back, clear as day. The boiled man had begged and cried. He'd used the name, and the beast had responded.

Hannah had been his sister.

The memories flooded back, and he began to relive the night. The beast had been cruel and cold, but he'd shown that he had a heart. He'd left Shaun alone. He'd heard Shaun's story. So why now? Why not kill him then when it was all set up? If Harvey *had* murdered Shaun back then, the misery of the past three years would never have happened. Shaun's mum might have recovered from her grief, and he would now just be a memory.

Maybe he'd even be missed.

Another pair of eyes stared at Shaun through his darkened mind, white and lifeless, yet rolling in their sockets, desperately searching for light. The boiling water had cooked them like eggs. The searing heat of the ancient bathtub had melted the skin of the man's arms to the copper. His flesh had peeled away in gloopy chunks as he'd frantically dabbed at his ruined eyes.

Yet the eyes had still roamed.

For a while, anyway.

Shaun wondered what manner of death the beast was

planning outside the van. The fire must be large, from the sound of the rush he'd heard, with hot fiery coals. How long had he been there? In the darkness, it was hard to tell. Amongst the fear, it was a lifetime.

A twig broke outside.

The side door was yanked open.

Shaun pounced from his crouched position and slashed at the beast with his small knife, who was standing silhouetted by the fire. Shaun caught him off guard. His hands shot up to defend himself, and Shaun felt the blade connect with skin. But he didn't look back. He landed and ran.

He ran past the fire into the trees, away from the light and into the darkness. He ran until he could barely see himself then he ran some more. The jelly-like feeling in his legs took hold like he was running in tar. He was sure he could hear the beast behind him. He needed to hide. The fire was small, maybe three hundred meters away. Shaun ducked behind a tree and searched the darkness for movement.

The thump of his heart and his breathing was loud in the quiet night, and holding his breath only made his heart beat louder.

Was he safe?

Should he wait there until light? Where was the road?

Shaun's breathing eased enough for him to begin to hear the noises in the trees. The scratching of a small mammal on the ground a way off. The rustle of the leaves in the gentle breeze. The occasional pop and crackle of the fire in the distance that sent sparks into the air.

But no other movement.

Shaun rose to his feet slowly. His eyes never left the direction from which he'd run. He hoped to see the silhouette of the beast, of Harvey. At least then, he would know which way to run.

He took a step back, keeping the tree between his body and the fire.

His heart started to pound once more, as he began to make his escape.

He was close to the edge of the trees. He could see the long grass beyond the forest that shimmered like water in the pale moonlight.

That was his escape.

"*Shaun.*"

He froze. His mouth was bone dry with fear. He was unable to swallow. The whisper had seemed to come from nowhere, yet everywhere.

He spun.

Darkness.

Had he imagined it?

The long grass beckoned. It was just forty feet away.

His head swivelled back and forth, searching the blackness for a sign, for a shape, for movement. Anything.

"*Shaun.*"

The hushed whisper had come from the grass.

There was nobody there.

"*Shaun.*"

No, it came from the trees.

The beast was all around.

He turned once more, stepping backwards, edging towards the grass, to safety, to anywhere, to nowhere.

Somewhere to run.

"*Shaun.*"

Behind him.

He spun.

Those eyes.

"Kill the lights," said Melody, as the camper approached the open wrought iron gates of John Cartwright's estate. "Drive straight past. We'll park further down the lane and walk back."

"We?" said Reg. "I thought I-"

"You've got two options, Reg," said Melody. "You can either stay here in the creepy dark lane all by yourself, knowing there's a serial killer out there." She turned to face him and saw the look of dread on his face. "Or you can come with Boon and me."

"You're taking the dog?"

"Of course I'm taking the dog. His eyes and ears are better than ours."

Reg pulled the camper to the side of the small lane and let out a long breath.

"I don't like this one bit," he said.

"And what about me?" said Melody. She opened her door. Her voice fell to a whisper. "You think I'm in love with this whole idea? A few days ago, I was talking about my wedding with my fiancé." She tucked her Sig into the back of her cargo pants and clicked her fingers for Boon to come. "Now I'm hunting him down."

"That puts things into perspective," said Reg, as he climbed down. He gently pushed the door closed and joined Melody in the lane.

"Just remember, you're his friend, he doesn't want to hurt you," whispered Melody, as they started to walk back up the lane towards the two iron gates.

"What if we're too late?" asked Reg. "What if-"

"We're not too late," interrupted Melody. "If I know Harvey as well as I think I do, he'll take his time with this one."

"Why?" asked Reg. "Why not just get the job done and get out of here? I mean if he's looking for closure-"

"He's looking for suffering," said Melody.

"Suffering?"

"Suffering, Reg." She stopped in the middle of the dark lane and explained in whispered tones. "The people he targets are sex offenders. They've destroyed lives. They're sick and twisted people, and each one of them represents the men who raped and killed his sister. To him, they're just as bad." Melody looked up into Reg's eyes to make sure he was following. "A quick death wouldn't bring the justice he's looking for. It wouldn't offer the retribution, and it wouldn't bring peace to Hannah's memory."

Reg nodded slowly. "I understand."

"So, let's go. Walk quietly."

They turned into the gates and hopped across the gravel to the much quieter grass.

"Didn't there used to be a house there?" asked Reg.

"Harvey burned it down," said Melody.

"Speaking of fire," said Reg, "look over there."

In the distance to their left, the tall flames of a large fire lit the surrounding area and the underside of the trees that bordered an orchard.

"It's the orchard. Of course. That's where his parents are buried."

"In an orchard?"

"Follow me," said Melody, ignoring his questions.

Melody walked slowly, keeping Boon by her side, and listening for him to alert her to anyone approaching in the darkness with his low growl. She'd always hated the place. It was large, old and creepy, and now that it had fallen into disrepair, the wild, overgrown gardens had begun to overcome everything that stood in its way. She took a wide path around the fire. Her eyes scanned the area for movement, for Harvey's shadow. She saw the black van parked nearby the fire, but no movement.

Melody lowered to a crouch, as she grew closer.

"Keep down, Reg," she whispered blindly.

The flames were large next to what looked like a huge pile of wood. But no sign of anyone tending the fire. He'd be near. He'd show himself. It was just a matter of time.

Maybe Tyson was still in the van? Maybe she could get him out.

She stopped beside a lone willow beside a trickling stream and turned back to Reg.

"Stay here," she whispered. "I'll be back for you. If you see anything, whistle."

Reg nodded with wide eyes. Melody could plainly see he was scared out of his mind. She handed him Boon's lead then pulled her Sig from her belt, and made her way slowly towards the van.

The long grass made staying quiet difficult, so she lowered herself to the ground, softly and quietly, and for the last hundred yards, she crawled.

One elbow.

One knee.

Push.

Scan for movement.

One elbow.

One knee.

Push.

It was slow going, and the thick grass obscured her view, but gradual progress was her safest option.

Melody drew close the van. The sound of the fire was loud and clear. She attuned herself to the environment. She tried to understand the noises, the crackle of wood, the gentle swish of grass as the soft breeze rolled across its tips in waves.

The thud of heavy wood hitting the ground.

Melody froze.

Another thud.

She peered beneath the van to the fire behind it.

Something dragged across the earth.

A rush of sparks flew high into the air, and the flames reached up higher than the van, just licking the lowest of the tree's outstretched limbs.

Footsteps.

Melody pulled the grass in around her.

Two black boots stopped in front of the fire. A garden spade slammed into the earth beside them.

She needed to move. She was too open.

One knee.

One elbow.

Push.

Stop.

She listened. The boots hadn't moved. If she could just get beneath the van, she'd be safer. She could watch him prepare. She might even understand him a little more.

Melody crawled forward, her eyes fixed on the boots. The space beneath the van was just large enough for her to squeeze in and lay on her front with her Sig ready to fire. She crawled in slowly and felt him there, a few feet away.

Beyond the boots, in the fire, Melody saw for the first time what the pile of wood had concealed.

Melody shuddered.

In the very core of the fire was the main act, with flames licking its sides greedily, and its cast iron claw feet embedded into the glowing hot coals like some kind of creature from hell.

The old copper bathtub.

18

A KISS FROM THE BEAST

"TURN HERE," SAID GEORGE, LOOKING AT THE MAP ON HIS smart phone. "The estate is on the left. That's it there, see the big iron gates?"

"Jesus," said Harris. "Would you look at this place?"

Harris pulled the car onto the gravel driveway, stopped, and killed the lights.

"We're on foot from here," he told George.

"Sir, do you think we should tell someone where we are?" asked George.

"What's the matter with you?" replied Harris. "You're not afraid of the dark are you?"

George huffed, and climbed out of the car.

They pushed the car doors closed quietly and began to move into the long grass.

"Sir," said George, "look over there. Fire."

Harris held the handgun down by his side. He fingered the safety catch, nodded in reply to George, and then began to move off slowly in a wide circle to the right of the fire.

He strode carefully through the grass, as quietly as he could, and keeping an eye on the fire for any sign of movement. He made it as far as the tree line at the edge of the orchard, and began to hug the shadows as he worked his way along towards the fire.

"George, do you see the van?" said Harris, "just through the trees there. Bingo, my friend. We're in the right place."

But George didn't reply.

Harris glanced back, but there was no sign of George.

"George?" he hissed.

Harris' eyes scanned back in the direction of the car, but there was no movement.

He carried on alone, and with his gun in front of him, he made straight for the van.

His footsteps were bolder. There was no need to be scared, he told himself. He *was* armed after all.

He raised the weapon, switched the safety off and worked his way along the tree line toward the fire. Stopping thirty metres from the van, he surveyed the darkness. Nothing but darkness.

Around the fire were five tall trees that formed a C shape that half-enclosed the area, creating a little clearing. A thick bough was standing out proudly from the largest and most central of the five trees, from which hung what looked to Harris like a heavy chain.

In the centre of the fire beneath the chain was a shape.

What was it?

He focused harder, trying to make out the shape. His night vision was ruined from staring at the bright firelight, but then the shape took form and Harris froze.

It was an old-fashioned bathtub.

His heart began to race.

Clearly, the killers had taken the time to set the scene up perfectly, but the lack of movement and noise added to the anxiety. He wiped his sweaty palms on his trousers and ran his tongue across his lips.

Should he approach? What if the killers were waiting in the trees? Who knew if they were also armed? Where was the camper?

He lowered to a crouch and scanned behind him for George. Harris sucked in a few deep breaths to calm himself, then stood and took two steps forward.

Something wasn't right.

He wasn't alone.

Slowly he turned his head and stared into the darkness of the trees beside him.

There was something in there.

He took a step closer.

Something shined briefly in the moonlight, so faint.

Teeth?

A smile?

Suddenly, a hand reached out of the darkness and clamped onto his throat.

Harris tried to call out, but there was no air.

He pulled at the hands but they were too strong, like iron, and sticky with blood.

Harris kicked, but was dizzy and weak.

He fought for breath.

The hand squeezed tighter.

A brief inhale of chemical.

Harris knew the smell.

But it was too late.

He dropped to the ground.

The two black boots took a small step back then swivelled sideways on one heel and one toe, like a soldier might begin a left turn. Then, they began to move as they made their way from the fire towards the orchard and disappeared into the long grass.

Melody shuffled forwards to see which way he'd headed. But in the darkness with just the dancing flames to light her surroundings, finding the shape was futile.

She tapped lightly on the underside of the van with her Sig. Three taps, slow, but enough to let him know he wasn't alone. She hoped Tyson would respond to let her know he'd heard.

He didn't reply. Why would he? He was probably tied up and gagged, sitting in the darkness terrified beyond imagination.

Melody would need to let Shaun out, but she didn't have much time. Who knew when Harvey would return and begin his gruesome plan? She took a couple of long breaths and planted her hands on the ground, ready to slide out backwards.

Suddenly, two hands grabbed her ankles. Two iron-like grips, strong and large. She inhaled sharply and gave a soft murmur. Wrenched backwards from her hiding place, she watched as the Sig slid from her grip and fell to the ground.

A hard knee pressed down and he forced her hands together behind her back.

"Harvey," she hissed, "it's me."

Harvey didn't reply.

Her hands were bound with cable ties that immediately began to dig into her skin.

"Ow, Harvey, what are you doing?"

Harvey didn't reply.

A canvas bag was forced over her head, and she heard the familiar zip of a cable tie fastening it tightly behind her neck.

"Stop it," she said. "I just want to help you."

Dragged to her feet, she tried to kick out at him, but her

arms were forced up behind her, nearly dislocating her shoulders.

"You're hurting me, Harvey," she hissed. "Just stop it."

Harvey didn't reply.

A gentle nudge encouraged her to start walking. She felt the heat of the fire to her left and imagined where she was being led. Powerful arms forced her against a tree then she heard the rattle of heavy chains.

"Harvey? What are you doing?" she said gently. "This is too far."

No reply.

"Harvey, just talk to me. Please?"

She was forced to turn around and the heavy chain was thrown around her neck. She knew it was coming, but when the chain pulled tight, she gasped at the feeling of it against her throat.

The click of a padlock added a tense finality to the silence.

She didn't even hear him leave.

Was he behind her still?

Had he moved off?

Then a stark reality hit home and her stomach rolled with disgust, fear and hatred. She'd been too confident of his feelings for her.

He was going to boil *her*.

"Harvey?" she said softly. "It's me. You're not going to hurt me." She tried to command him.

But silence.

"Is anyone there?" she called out, louder this time. "Help."

The heat from the fire a few yards away warmed her skin and her neck prickled. She could feel a bead of sweat run down her chest.

This is fear. Don't be afraid.

But her inner strength was forced to the back of her mind

by the muffled whimpers of someone close by. Something was dragged to the tree beside her. A man cried out in the darkness. He begged for mercy, and chains rattled once more.

Was that Reg?

Melody guessed he would be hooded and fixed to a tree just as she had been.

"Harvey, you're out of control," she shouted blindly. "This is it. This is the end. It's over."

Harvey didn't reply.

"Who's there?" said a man's voice, thickened from his tears.

That's not Reg, she thought.

"Don't worry," replied Melody. "This isn't over yet. Just hang in there."

"I can't die," he said. "I have a family. I have children."

"Take it easy," whispered Melody. "Try to control your breathing."

The man took several breaths.

"That's it," said Melody. "Just relax. If he wanted you dead, you'd be dead by now."

"Somehow I find that hard to believe," he replied.

"What's your name?"

"George, Dave George."

"You're police?" asked Melody.

"Yes, how did you-"

"It was me. I shot your tyre," said Melody. Somehow, honesty seemed a way to induce trust with her condemned companion.

"You?" he said. His breathing began to ramp up again. "But you-"

"Easy, calm down," said Melody. "You shouldn't have come here."

George took a few more breaths and then sobbed loudly from inside his canvas hood. "I know, I didn't want to, but-"

"But what?" asked Melody. "Your boss? He's here too?"

George didn't respond.

"Is he armed?" asked Melody, quietly.

George began to reply, but once more, the silence was broken by the sound of something else being dragged across the ground in front of them. The familiar rattle of chains clattered in the night.

The click of a padlock.

Once more, no footsteps of him walking away.

Was he close?

She spoke in hushed whispers, blind to her surroundings.

"Who's that?" whispered Melody.

No reply.

"Harris?" said George. "Is that you?"

"George?" came the muffled and groggy reply.

"Sir, are you okay?"

"Not really, George, no."

"Are you chained to a tree?" asked George.

"And hooded," he confirmed.

"I'm guessing you both are too?" said Harris.

Melody didn't reply.

"How many of us?" asked Harris. "Do we know?"

"Three of us, as far as I can make out," said Melody. "I don't suppose you boys bothered to call uniforms for backup?"

"How do you know we're police?"

"She shot our tyre, sir."

"She what?" said Harris, louder than he meant to. He lowered his voice to a hiss. "It was you? In the camper?"

"You shouldn't have come," replied Melody flatly. "This isn't the place for a small town detective. You're in way over your heads."

"Tell me something I don't know," said Harris.

Melody heard him test the chains and then succumb to the fact that he was stuck.

"Hang on," said George. "The camper? There were two of you. Where's the driver? The small guy?"

Something landed on the ground to their left with a thud.

It began to whimper.

"Reg, you're okay. You're with us."

She was quietened by a hard hit to the side of her face.

The temptation to call out to Harvey was strong, but the two police didn't need to know about their relationship. It would cause distrust, and right now, they needed to stay together.

Reg moaned as he too was bound to the tree with chains.

"Melody?" he called. "Are you there?"

"We're here, Reg," she replied. "Don't worry. We're all here."

"The detectives?" he asked hopefully.

"We're here," they both said at once.

"I don't suppose you-"

"Called backup?" finished Harris. "No, I'm afraid not."

The sound of a spade digging into the ground silenced them all. Melody tried hard to see through the tiny holes in the canvas, but it was no use. He was digging. A rhythm built up somewhere to Melody's left, beside the fire.

A sharp rasp, as the spade sank into the earth. A dirty crunch, as it was forced backwards. Then the scatter of dirt onto a pile.

A hole?

To bury them all?

She fought back tears and a small part of her was thankful for the hood. She didn't need the men to see her cry.

It's not over yet. She told herself.

George began to cry again. Melody heard him quietly. She

heard him try to refrain, to hold it in, but he'd broken with a loud sob and the gates had opened.

It was too much for Melody.

"You pig," she spat.

The digging stopped.

"I thought you were better than this," she continued. "But you're not. You're just a cold-blooded killer. You deserve to go to prison. You deserve to rot in hell."

She felt him stand in front of her. His presence darkened the limited light that the canvas allowed. Melody trembled. She no longer knew the man who was standing in front of her.

She could hear his breathing.

"Stop," she whispered, so only he could hear. "It's not too late."

She felt a finger on her throat, below the thick chain that held her bound to the tree.

"What are you doing?" she said. A soft unintentional whimper followed. She tried to move away, to slide up and down, anywhere, just away from his touch.

His finger lowered and caught on the neck of her shirt.

"Stop."

He pulled.

"No," she began to beg. "No, no more, just stop."

The shirt began to rip.

Melody cried out.

"Melody, what's happening?" It was Reg.

"Nothing, Reg," said Melody, her voice nearly an octave higher than normal. "Just be cool."

Her shirt fell open, and she felt the warmth of the fire on her skin.

His soft touch ran across her chest.

Tears came silently inside her hood, and she lowered her head.

She was powerless against him. He'd opened her up, he exposed her deepest fears and now flaunted them.

She began to visibly shake.

Her knees buckled, but her throat hung on the chains and forced her to stand straight.

His finger lifted her chin.

"Please, Harvey," she whispered. "No more. It's too much."

He stepped closer.

The shape grew darker.

He kissed her through the thick canvas.

19

A GAME OF PAIN

HARRIS FELT A TUG AT THE BACK OF HIS HOOD AND HEARD the clip of cutters on the cable tie, then felt the canvas hood pulled roughly from his head. He breathed in the cool air with an open mouth and groaned.

The hot coals in front were bright on his eyes. He looked down, trying to focus on the ground. There wasn't much to see, just tufts of grass and mud, and a wash of orange that grew and faded with rhythmic intensity.

The man had slipped away, back into the trees as silently as he'd come. Harris was glad. He tried to turn his head to see the tree beside him, but the chains were tight on his throat. All he saw were shapes, four of them.

To his right was open grassland. Beyond the fire, the soft tips of wild grass ebbed and flowed with the breeze, the breeze that he now breathed with pleasure. A man groaned to his left, far away, the furthest tree maybe. But Harris couldn't see. Another groan of pleasure.

Another hood removed?

Who was it? Was it George?

"Tell us what's happening at least," called Harris to their captor.

The killer.

"Tell us *why*."

The killer didn't reply.

The faint sound of the cutters travelling through the air and the sound of another canvass hood being ripped off a head. Another sound of temporary joy and the sharp intake of air.

That's three of us, he thought.

"George, are you there?" called Harris.

"I am, sir," came the reply.

Harris closed his eyes. He'd got George into this; it was on him. If George died, Harris would die. He wouldn't be able to face George's family and tell them what had happened and why.

Why was it happening?

It had all snowballed. Harris saw it now, clear as day. He'd made a connection, George had added solidity to his theory, and now, they were both tied to a tree before a fire with a hideous ancient copper bathtub that was almost glowing with heat.

The fire had died down.

Red hot coals shimmered like the fires of hell, and Harris was lost in the movement of light. He imagined the saddened faces of George's children. He imagined Susan's face. The devastation. The shame.

And all the time, why?

"He idolised you," she would say. "He would have followed you anywhere, and you should have known. You should have called for backup."

It's my fault.

Harris craned his neck to find George. But at the furthest

reach of his neck, he saw only blurred and dark shadows standing waiting by trees.

Snip.

The final hood was ripped off, and the girl sucked in the cool air just as he had, as they all had.

"Are you okay?" he asked when the shadow had slipped back into the darkness.

"You talk when I tell you to talk," came a harsh whisper from behind his right ear.

It had been almost silent, like the wind or some drug-fuelled imagining.

But it had been real.

Harris took deep breaths, closed his eyes, and calmed his racing heart. The man was obviously sick. Things were out of control.

Was this really his fault?

He thought of his own wife, Patricia, and wondered if she'd be devastated. Harris knew she'd be upset, as any wife might be. But devastated? Not like Susan. In some ways, his death might be a release for her. A release from the grind of daily life they'd developed. A release from the monotonous routine of courteous manners, asking the right questions at the right time, and not doing certain things to upset the other, or doing other things just to save an argument.

That had been when he'd known his marriage was over, the day he realised that the reason he did certain things for Patricia had turned from enjoying the look of joy on her face to preventing the look of disappointment.

The thick chain that hung from the tree trailed out on the ground beside the fire. It began to pull tight as someone slowly pulled on the loose end.

Harris heard the girl beside him, who was lost to his peripheral vision, begin to question what was happening.

She called him Harvey.

Did she know him?

He failed to see the connection between the camper and the killer. Who were they? What were they doing here? Were they helping him? Were they trying to stop him?

The girl was released from the tree in a clatter of chains and shoved forward onto her knees. Harris saw her face for the first time since she'd looked down the length of the rifle.

The rifle.

It had been military grade. It wasn't an ordinary *dad's got a gun* type of rifle; it had been heavy firepower.

A big black boot sprang from nowhere and kicked her in the side.

She didn't move.

She was tough.

Maybe she was military. Maybe they'd been undercover and George and him had been in the way. Maybe that was why they had shot the tyre, to keep them away. But he'd been greedy. George had protested, and he hadn't listened.

It's your fault.

The man wore a hood to hide his face and stepped from the darkness. He pulled on the chain that hung from the thick bough above and fastened it around her neck. Then he dropped a single white envelope onto the ground beside her, before stepping back into the darkness.

"What is it?" whispered Harris. "What does it say?"

She looked up at him. Her tangled flock of curly brown hair hung limply on her shoulders, and her top was ripped open, revealing a white bra. But she didn't seem to care. She didn't try to cover herself.

Had she lost her own fight?

The girl slid a slender finger into the envelope, ripped the paper then pulled the note out. She let the discarded envelope drift with the breeze into the hot coals, where it shimmered and shuddered before curling and burning.

And then it was consumed.

The girl read the note to herself, and then stared at each of the men in turn.

"*So?*" said Harris. "*Read it to us.*"

The girl's eyes hung lazily on his.

"What does it say, Melody?" called the other guy, the driver.

Her head turned slowly to face her friend. But then it dropped and hung low, and she let her hand fall to her side. A deathly silence hung in the air as all three men anxiously waited for the girl to speak, their eyes pleading for news, anything, good news, bad news. But Harris' heart knew it would not be pleasant.

The girl took another single short look at all three men once more, just quickly, no eye contact. Then she returned her stare to the note in her hand.

"It's a game," she said.

———

Shaun was sitting cross-legged with his arms and legs tied around the tree in front of him with what felt like strips of material. His head rested on the rough bark, which hurt his skin, but he no longer cared. The time for caring about pain was over. The time for escape had passed.

It was his time to die.

At the back of his mind, the idea that his mum would never know this pain he endured eased him. The three years he'd spent crying and wishing he was different had just delayed the suffering process.

The beast had been waiting for him.

It was him. It was the same man. Shaun had seen the eyes. Just like in his dreams. Those cold eyes had shone from the darkness. His strong hands had held him until any morsel of help had been squeezed from his fragile mind.

He wished the end would come soon.

The beast had disappeared into the darkness and left him alone. Somehow, being alone with his thoughts was worse. At least when somebody was near, he wasn't alone.

Shaun heard screams somewhere close by, and a woman shouting, but the tape across his mouth muffled his efforts to join in the cries.

Maybe he wasn't alone in death.

If there was one, maybe there were more. Maybe the beast would offer him a chance of living again, just like before.

Maybe not.

More shouting rang through the trees and fell silently away. No reply came.

No help would come.

"Do you know who I am?" said the beast quietly from behind him in the darkness.

Shaun startled and shook his head. Where did he come from? How is he so quiet?

"But you recognise me?"

Shaun squeezed his eyes shut tight, and shook his head.

"I don't want to know," he mumbled through the tape.

"Do you remember, Shaun?" said the beast. "Do you remember that night?"

Shaun was breathing hard through his nose. He nodded softly, reluctantly.

"So you know who I am then?"

Shaun was silent.

"Do you know why I killed that man that night, Shaun?"

The beast was talking softly, not menacingly and not kindly, just softly.

Shaun nodded.

"You heard his story, didn't you?"

Shaun nodded again.

"Who do you fear the most, Shaun?" asked the beast. "Yourself, with your afflictions, or me, with my own afflictions?"

Shaun shrugged his shoulders.

The beast stepped out from behind Shaun and began to pace around him. He disappeared into the darkness in front then emerged behind him.

"Why do you think I let you go, Shaun?"

Shaun searched the space behind him, but the beast had moved, vanished into the trees.

He shrugged.

"You were supposed to be my last."

Tears flowed from Shaun's eyes. He wished the beast would just finish him. He wished he'd stop the games. The beast spoke like they were old friends, or like they somehow shared a common affliction or weakness.

The beast lowered himself to the ground beside Shaun, crouched on one knee.

"Do you think this is easy for me, Shaun?"

Shaun stared wide-eyed.

"Do you think that taking a life is satisfying?"

Shaun didn't reply.

"Do you think I'm evil?"

Shaun looked away.

The beast seemed somehow disappointed in his response. It was almost as if behind those cold eyes was a heart, or a genuine desire to be liked. He turned to face him again and understood.

"People think you're evil, Shaun. Yet you try so hard not to be. Do the voices inside you battle over good and bad, Shaun?"

Shaun nodded.

"Is it like the goodness inside you tries to keep the evil away?"

Shaun nodded. He was breathing hard and wanted the tape to be removed from his mouth so he could reply.

Somebody understood.

"Do you ever wonder if the good will win the battle?" said the beast. "Or does some part of you realise that no matter how hard you try, no matter what good you do, the evil inside you will strike when you're weak, and destroy everything you've worked for?

Shaun nodded softly, blinked once, and let the tears roll.

"Do you want to beat it?"

20

SACRIFICE

MELODY KNELT ON THE GROUND WITH THE HOT COALS warming her back and the note in her hand. A shadow passed through the trees in front of her, behind the men. He was silent. He was toying with them, and now the end was near.

To her right was a large hole, more like a grave, only half as deep. But deep enough for a body or even four.

"Tell us what it says," said the detective, the one in charge.

His voice stirred Melody from a daze. So much had happened, and there was so much yet to come.

"We're all going to die," said Melody, softly and with a hint of acceptance.

The three men all reacted in their own way.

She looked up at the second detective, who emitted a high-pitched whine that turned into a sob and then full on crying, like how a child might cry. She felt for him. Harvey used to say that fear was stage one in the process.

The detective on her far left became angry. Harvey would be watching from the shadows, and he would call that stage two.

She couldn't look at Reg. But she heard him breathing loudly, controlling his thoughts. Reg wasn't a tough guy, but he'd seen enough of Harvey to know that this was real. Reg was at stage three, acceptance.

"How?" spat the man on the far left. "How is he going to kill us? He can't boil us all."

Melody pulled at the chain around her neck and noted the length.

It was perfect.

She looked around the scene and saw the last tree, empty of prisoners, and she thought of Shaun. Maybe that was where he was supposed to have been standing. Why wasn't he there?

Melody glanced into the angry water that simmered in the bathtub. It was dark, but she could see the water was clear, not bloody. Shaun hadn't been boiled before they'd arrived.

The van.

"Are you going to talk to us?" said the man on the left. "We deserve to know."

Melody snapped back to the game.

"I have to choose one person," she said.

"Choose?" said the man. "What do you mean, choose?"

"One of us will be dropped into the tub, and I have to choose who."

"What if you don't choose?"

"Then it's me that boils," said Melody bluntly.

"And the rest of us?"

Melody took a deep breath and sank lower onto her knees.

"I have to kill two of you," said Melody. "The third person..."

She looked back at the fire and stared transfixed at the claw-foot tub.

She felt Reg's eyes boring into her. She turned to face him.

Their eyes met. An understanding passed silently between them.

A single tear ran from Melody's eye.

"So you get to live?" asked the man on the left. "You get to go free after this?'

"Free?" snapped Melody. "Do you realise what I've been told to do? Do you think that by doing this, I'll somehow skip out of here and live happily ever after?"

"You know him," he replied. "You said his name. I heard you. It was you in the camper, you shot at us, and you're part of this, him as well." He gestured at Reg, who had hung his head low but flinched at the attack. "And where's the pervert? Is he in the van? Isn't that for him?" He nodded at the bathtub in the coals.

"You don't get it, do you?" spat Melody. "You don't understand that I have to choose two people to kill. I have to take their lives." Her voice broke. "Two of you get to die quickly." She paused. "And one of you will die a slow and painful death." She stared at the tub and the grass beyond, which was blurred by heat. "You're making it harder for me not to let that one person be you."

"*I'm* making it harder for *you*?" said the man. "Am I supposed to-"

"Shut up," shouted George. "Just shut the hell up." He fought to crane his neck, but couldn't turn his head far enough to see his boss. "It was *you* who wanted to come here, it was you that wanted the glory, and it was you who said not to call for backup. So just shut the hell up. We're in this together. If anyone needs to boil, it's you."

"Reg?" said Melody. "What do you think?"

Reg kept his head down low. It took a few moments for him to respond, and when he did, he could manage only one mumbled sentence.

"I don't want to die, Melody."

"How are you going to do it?" asked the man on the left. His voice had dropped to a monotone tenor. The fight inside him seemed to have vanished.

Melody noted the change in his attitude and dismissed the man's temper as nerves, fear and the unknown. She'd taken various courses when she worked on the force. Hostage situations and post-terrorist attacks were prone to elicit various forms of emotions from people. Dealing with them required a certain amount of emotional intelligence. What they hadn't taught her was that when her own life was in danger, she'd have to deal with her own fears, thoughts and demons too, as well as those of others.

"My bare hands, I guess," she replied.

George broke the silence that followed.

"You think you can do that?" he asked.

Melody set the note on the ground.

"It wouldn't be the first time," she said, quietly. "And he *knows* it. He's testing me."

"Testing you?" said George. "Don't you think it's a test for all of us? I mean, after all, we're all chained up here. Maybe he's watching us, analysing us."

Melody shook her head. "No," she said, and pushed herself up to her feet. "He's testing me. He's pushing me."

"You two are close?" asked the man on the left. "You know his name."

"Yeah, we're close. We *were* close, once upon a time."

"So get through to him. Talk to him." He was almost pleading. "Can't you do something?"

The chain around Melody's neck suddenly moved. It was being pulled up.

"I'm running out of time."

"So kill me," said the man. He stopped as soon as he'd said it, and realised the gravity of his words.

"It's not as easy as that."

The chain crept another link over the thick bough.

"What did it say?" asked Reg. "The note. Read it to us."

Melody fumbled with the paper. Her hands shook, and she could barely make out the words with just the light from the coals.

"It's just what I said," said Melody. "Kill two and one will boil. Then below, it says, or I'll be the first to go."

"Holy crap," said Reg. He was beginning to panic. "Melody, I trust you. Do what you need to do." He gave her a long hard look. "I don't think any of us are getting out of here."

"But how do I decide?" asked Melody. "Who am I to say who deserves to die slowly?"

Another link crept over the bough.

Melody held it tightly in her hand and stepped back to gauge the length of her leash.

"I think it reaches all of you, but the longer I wait, the harder it'll be."

Another link.

Melody glanced at the bathtub.

"I choose me," she said. "I can't decide."

"Melody, no," said Reg. "We don't even know how he's going to kill you, or what he's going to do with us when he's done."

"He's right," said the man on the left. "If you can't decide, and he puts you in the water, we might all face the same fate. Who knows?"

"Melody," said Reg, "surely it's better to finish two of us on our terms? Not his."

"How about drawing straws?" said George. "We each pick some grass, and the shortest one-"

"Dies horribly?" finished Melody. "No way. That's not on our own terms."

Another link.

"Oh my God. I can't do this."

"Just get on with it, you fucking bitch," shouted the man on the left.

Melody was taken back by the attack and began to respond, but he continued with his insult.

"You know you want to save your friend, so there's one of the two. Now all you need to do is choose between George and me. Well, I'm making it easy for you. Give George the easy way out. I'll do it. I'll be the one. I'll take the short straw. I deserve it, he doesn't. This was my idea. I talked him into it. So just get on with it and stop pitying yourself."

He turned away from her, panting slightly from the emotional outburst, to let his own words sink in.

"I'll be the one," he repeated quietly. "I won't hear another word on it."

21

FIRE

HARRIS LET HIS HEAD DROP.

He wished there was some way he could end it all himself. Maybe he could strangle himself with the chain? But he could barely move, and as much as the chain dug into his throat and caused him to gag, that would be the extent of it.

He began to twist and wrench his body away out of frustration. No control. Why should someone else be the one who dictates how he dies?

And the girl? The bitch was making it sound like she had a choice, making it sound like it was some kind of hardship for her. What would happen if she did kill two of them and save one for the tub?

She was in on it.

The more he thought about it, the more it made sense. She was sitting on the ground with the note looking sorry for herself. How did they even know what was written on the paper? She could have said anything.

Another link rolled over the bough, and her leash grew smaller still. Pretty soon, she wouldn't be able to reach them, and who knew what that meant.

"Just hurry the fuck up, will you?" he shouted. "You're making it harder for all of us. If we're going to die, then just bloody do it."

He wished he could see her face, but a part of him was grateful for not being able to see George. He doubted he'd be able to look him in the eye. He couldn't bear the look of hate, of blame.

It's all your fault.

"You want to be the one?" she asked. "Are you sure about that?"

Her voice was authoritative. She was a leader. Her tone was flat, but she was in control, and she knew it.

Another link.

Then a thud.

"What was that?" he asked her. "What just happened?"

"I know how I'm supposed to do it," the girl replied.

"Well, are you going to tell us?"

Instead of replying, she stood. He heard the chains rattling and her shuffling feet, bound at the ankles.

She approached him and stopped directly in front of him.

The chain was nearly at its full length.

Harris admired her. She was strong, very pretty, and with her shirt torn open, he could see how fit she was.

She held up a knife.

"You wanted to see?" she said. "This is how it ends."

A knife. There it was. She could end it all right now.

"Come closer," he whispered. His eyes darted back to the others and then returned to hers.

She stepped forward and leaned in so he could whisper in her ear.

"You're a pretty one," he said, his eyes fixed on her chest. In the dark, the white of her bra seemed to glow. "How about you give me one last request and show me what you have in there?"

The girl's face tightened. She stepped back half a step.

"Or maybe even a kiss," he said.

A look of disgust.

"Or maybe more. Come on, it'll be our last time. You have such pretty lips."

Her arm swung up and over her shoulder.

Harris instinctively flinched, shut his eyes, and waited for the pain. Nothing but the thud of the blade digging into the tree.

"There's nothing more I'd like," she whispered, "than to sink this blade into your head."

Another link reminded them of time.

"So do it," he snapped. "Just bloody end it."

"An easy death for you means a harder death for someone else, and right now, if anyone deserves a slow and painful death, it's you."

She began to step backwards, holding the chain away from her feet with one hand and the knife in the other. That was it. That had been his chance, his only chance at antagonising her into ending it all for him.

Now he would surely boil.

The chain seemed to be shortening faster as if Harvey was growing more impatient as time went by.

Melody needed to make a choice.

For the briefest of moments, the thought of suicide crossed her mind. But she knew that all men would suffer for her cowardice. She couldn't let Reg suffer. She somehow felt responsible for him, for this.

He'd be at home with Jess if it weren't for her.

Melody doubted he would ever see Jess again. But if he

was going to die, he was right, they should all die on their own terms.

She also considered running from man to man, a quick slice of the jugular, exactly how Harvey had shown her, and they would die quickly.

But Melody knew that he'd tighten the chain before she reached the last man. He deserved to boil anyway. She knew he was playing her, trying to provoke her into using the knife. But she owed it to Reg and George. She owed them a clean, quick death.

But who to do first?

She stopped between Reg and George, glanced up at them, but turned away.

Could she really do this?

"Me," said Reg. "Start with me."

It was as if he'd read her mind, as she battled to make the first move.

George's face began to screw up and he sobbed loudly. Shame, pride and dignity had long since vanished. All that remained was a condemned man. He'd been reduced to a snivelling wreck.

Melody pulled her chain and took the few steps toward Reg, whose face was downcast with his eyes closed as if waiting for her to just do what had to be done.

Another link.

Reg was at arm's length now. She could reach his neck. But she wished she could hug him, tell him she'd see him on the other side, thank him for being a friend, and for all the times they'd had together.

She thought of his smiling face. He'd always been happy, always been the one to make jokes, no matter how inappropriate.

He opened his eyes, looked up at her and nodded.

Another link.

She was running out of time.

"Do it," he croaked.

She wanted to reach out and smooth his hair, touch his face, anything. Just feel. Just let him know how she felt. To ease him.

To ease her.

Another link.

She reached out with the knife and set it on his neck. All she needed to do was push and slice. The knife handle was slippery in her sweaty hands and they trembled in the night.

"Do it, Melody," he said with urgency.

Another link.

The point of the blade pressed into his skin, and he lifted his head. He was ready.

"I love you, Reg."

Tears rolled freely from his eyes and he began to pant.

"Just get out of here, Melody," he said. "Do it, save yourself, and get out of here."

"I don't think that's-"

"Just let me have that thought, Melody," he said softly between sharp, heavy breaths. "Just let me think you're going to be okay."

Melody closed her eyes. She felt his neck through the knife. She could see it in her mind's eye.

She pushed harder.

Another link rolled over the bough.

She pushed harder, but her trembling hand fought to hold the knife.

"Do it, Melody," shouted Reg.

She pushed. But she couldn't grip the handle, as if her subconscious was holding her back.

"Melody, do it," said Reg. "Just push."

"I can't," she said, her voice high and broken.

Another link.

"Now, Melody."

"I can't."

"Reg gritted his teeth and forced his neck forward as far as the chains would allow, but the knife slipped through Melody's hand.

It fell to the ground.

He stared at her in disbelief. His jaw hung open as if realising for the first time that it would be his friend who suffered the most. It would be her that they would all watch die horrifically.

Another link rolled over the bough, then another, and another. Faster and faster, the slack chain began to tighten, and then pull on her neck. Melody stumbled backwards, fell to the ground, and gasped for air.

The chain grew tighter still. It began to choke her and pull her towards the fire and the evil bathtub.

Melody fought back, trying to grip the ground with her feet. But the chain was relentless. It seemed to drag her with ease. She felt the heat on her head and tried to roll away. But each time she tried, the chain pulled tighter until eventually, and at the base of its arc, it began to lift her into the air.

The pulling was smooth at first, but as more weight hung from the biting links of steel, the pulling turned to harsh jerks.

Her head was soon above the red-hot coals. The skin on her neck prickled and began to burn. She felt it tighten and smelled her hair as it began to give in to the heat.

Melody was choking. She allowed her body to fall limp but clung desperately to the chain that was cutting into her throat. Air was barely getting through, but she sucked as hard as she could.

She dizzied.

Another pull of the chain and Melody lifted higher, so

high she could see into the bathtub now, and the darkness beyond.

The chain grew tighter still. She rose higher.

Brightly coloured dots began to dance across her vision in long kaleidoscopic swirls as if her very soul was preparing to leave.

The long grass ahead appeared inviting somehow, soft, lush, and natural. But there was more. There was movement amongst the grass. Slowly but surely, a shadow grew larger.

The chain pulled tighter.

Shouting, distant and muffled.

A wave of black passed before her eyes.

Voices.

No air now.

Footsteps nearby.

It was close. She felt the warmth of death's embrace.

A man.

Darkness.

22

THE END OF AN ERA

HARVEY SCOOPED MELODY UP IN HIS ARMS AND TOOK THE weight off the chain, standing on the hot coals, holding her above the copper bathtub.

"I'm here," he shouted. "I'm here."

He stared into the darkness of the trees, past the open-mouthed men who were standing wide-eyed and aghast. His vision scanned the shadows for movement.

"It's me you want. Let her down," he called out. "Come and get me."

Harvey loosened the chain from Melody's throat with one hand while supporting her head.

"Let her down," he screamed again.

Suddenly, the chain began to loosen. Harvey stepped away from the hot coals that had begun to melt the soles of his boots and lowered Melody down to the ground.

She lay unconscious, and thin rasps of breath were the only indication she was alive, but barely.

Harvey found the padlock behind Melody's neck.

"Keys."

He left no room for debate.

"If you want *me*, throw me the keys, or you get no-one at all."

A gunshot rang out, and Harvey felt a punch to his shoulder, sharp and hot. He stumbled back to the ground, but scrambled back to Melody, clutching his wounded shoulder.

"*Keys.*"

A pair of keys on a ring landed in the grass beside him.

Harvey fumbled with the padlock, desperate to release the chain from Melody's neck. The keys slipped in his hands, but then the lock snapped open with a click. He frantically pulled it away, tossed it behind him into the fire, then loosened the chain and freed her throat.

Melody was unconscious still, but a faint pulse gave a small glimmer of hope.

Another gunshot, another punch, another run of hot, sticky blood. This time, it was his other shoulder.

Harvey moved back away from Melody and slowly rose like a condemned man with his arms outstretched as much as his new wounds would allow.

"You have me," he called out. "Now show your face and finish me like a real man."

Harvey glanced across at Reg, who seemed to smile at his presence. Harvey gave him a little nod.

"Come on," he shouted, working himself up, preparing himself for death. "I'm ready. Come and get me."

He stood tall, panting from pain, adrenaline and anger. A rage he'd fought so hard to control over the years, a force so powerful it had taken years of training to suppress, now coursed through him. It was as if, in death, it would be the rage that eventually took him down.

"Come on," he shouted again. "Where are you?"

"Put the chain around your neck," said the voice from the trees.

Harvey placed the voice directly in front of him. A London accent, almost familiar, but not quite.

"You can't get me without chains?" shouted Harvey. "After all you've done? You need chains to take me down?"

"I don't need chains, Stone," said the man. "I want the chains."

A cruel laugh rang out, cold and bitter. "I want to see you suffer, Stone. That's all I want. I want to see you suffer, and then I want to watch you die slowly." He paused and dropped the tone of his voice. "I want to put an end to Harvey Stone, once and for all."

"So show yourself," said Harvey. "Let's get this moving."

Melody began to cough and rolled onto her side.

"The chain, Stone," said the voice.

Harvey pulled the chain towards him and wrapped the slack end around his neck.

"There," he called, "it's done. Now show yourself."

The chain was suddenly pulled hard and fast, and snapped tight against Harvey's neck. He gasped for breath. He'd left room to breathe, but the chain had tightened and now closed off much of his airway. He gripped the links that dug into his throat, fighting for air.

Then slowly but surely, the shape of a man stepped from the shadows. He stopped on the edge of darkness like death himself.

"You should have died a long time ago, Stone."

Harvey didn't reply.

"So much death. Think of all the pain and suffering you've caused."

Harvey didn't reply.

"How many, do you think?" asked the shadow. "Fifty? A hundred? More?"

Harvey didn't reply.

"Tell us about them, Stone."

"About what exactly?" replied Harvey.

"Which one was your favourite?"

Harvey didn't reply.

"Stuck for words, eh?" said the man.

"My favourite?" said Harvey, through gritted teeth, standing on tiptoes, striving to keep his airway open. "It was a scene just like this."

"Do go on," said the man in the trees.

"But it was *you* with a noose around your neck, and not me."

"You must be mistaken," came the reply. "I don't recall ever being in such a position."

"You've had a noose around your neck ever since I saved your sorry ass."

The shadow didn't reply.

He stepped from the trees into the light of the fire.

"Jackson?" said Reg in surprise. "But, you-"

"Quiet, Tenant," said Jackson, without turning. "If you hadn't worked it out already, you're in the wrong job."

He stepped up to Harvey.

"But *you* worked it out just fine, didn't you?" he said.

"It wasn't hard," said Harvey.

"So tell me. Entertain us all with your insight."

"You had the access."

"I did," agreed Jackson.

"You had the means."

Jackson nodded.

"And, out of everyone out there, you wanted me dead more than anybody."

"Very good," said Jackson. "And for what reason?"

Harvey's feet were tiring. He was struggling to keep the chain loose enough to breathe.

"I'm a risk to you," Harvey began. "I saw you kill. If anyone can bring you down, it's me."

"You would have made a good operative, Stone," said Jackson. "You think like a villain."

Harvey didn't reply.

"You are a villain, Stone."

"So it was you all along?" said Reg. "It was you that killed-"

"Like I said, Tenant, if you can't keep up with the conversation, best you keep quiet, eh?"

"You bastard, sir," spat Reg.

Jackson's eyes didn't leave Harvey's face.

"You win some, you lose some, right Stone?" said Jackson. "Isn't that what you told somebody a long time ago?"

"Moments before you tortured him?" said Harvey. "Yeah, it was something like that."

"I'd love to stay and chat, but you know I have a busy morning ahead. It'll be light soon. Besides, we don't want your bath to get cold, do we?"

"Jackson?" rasped Harvey.

Jackson turned back to face Harvey.

"Any last words, Stone?"

"Come closer."

Harvey fought for breath, and stumbled onto the coals, causing a flash of angry sparks to jump from the fire.

Jackson waited for Harvey to stop swinging and steady himself, and then stepped forward.

"Any regrets, Stone?" he asked.

Harvey smiled.

"How did you know where we'd be?" asked Harvey.

"Oh come on, Stone," he replied. "I've been listening to Tenant's calls now for more than a year." He laughed to himself. "You should hear some of the things your girlfriend has to say about you, Harvey. They're like two old women."

"That was you in Athens too, wasn't it?" asked Harvey. "It was you behind it all."

"You've been a marked man for years, Stone. Don't be offended."

Harvey was struggling with the intense heat. His neck was swelling in the grip of the steel chain.

"I'm not offended," said Harvey. "But I do like to have a good reason when I kill a man. It pleases my moral compass, Jackson."

"What do you mean?" said Jackson, his head cocked and intrigued.

"I have to give it to you, Jackson," said Harvey, "this is a fantastic set up you have here, even by my standards."

"What are you talking about, Stone?"

"But for all your planning and eavesdropping, you forgot one important point."

Harvey smiled.

"I told you before that your last word will always be the one that kills you."

Harvey gave a short sharp whistle.

Jackson's eyes widened with fear.

"Boon?"

A sudden look of doubt and fear wiped the smug look from his face, just before Boon leapt from his full speed run, launched himself up and sunk his teeth into Jackson's neck.

23

FLY BEAST FLY

MELODY WOKE WITH THE RHYTHMIC BEAT OF HER HEART loud in her ears, and the stinging of burnt and scratched skin to remind her she was alive. She opened her eyes from the darkness that had welcomed her with its inviting warmth to see the black sky and shadows of the trees overhead.

Men were talking nearby. They weren't shouting. The conversation wasn't heated, but hatred ran thick in the tones of their voices.

A familiar friend rested his head on Melody's chest. His ears pricked up when Melody began to raise her head, and his tail thumped the ground when she smiled at him.

Was it a dream?

She searched her surroundings.

Reg was still chained to the tree. But he smiled at her in the dim light with genuine relief.

Her vision blurred with every movement of her head, but the two other men were still there too. George and his boss, the angry man. She tried to wipe her hair from her eyes, but her hands had been bound once more behind her back.

Melody tried hard to remember what had happened. She

was being pulled. Her neck still stung. She'd fought for breath, and she'd felt death beside her.

But now? Was this real?

"It's time, Jackson."

It was Harvey's voice.

"Harvey?" said Melody. "It's time to stop this." She winced at the pain in her temple when she spoke.

Harvey didn't reply.

"Let me down, Stone."

That's Jackson, she thought

"Jackson," said Melody. Though her eyes failed to focus, she stared blindly in the direction of his voice. "Jackson help us."

"Please, Stone," said Jackson. "You don't understand. Melody tell him. Tell him to stop."

Slowly the scene began to focus, and Melody rolled to her side to take it all in.

Jackson now hung above the old copper bathtub. A great loop of the chain had been fastened around his chest and under his arms. His head fell forward and his bound feet tried in vain to avoid the heat and steam that grew angrily from below.

"I understand, Jackson," said Harvey. "If *anybody* understands, it's *me*."

Harvey stepped into view.

"Harvey?" said Melody. "Is that you? It's time to stop now. No more. Please."

Harvey bent and smoothed the hair on her forehead then planted a light kiss on her smooth skin.

"*This* is my last," said Harvey, then smiled weakly.

Melody watched with fear and astonishment as the man she loved began to circle Jackson like a wolf might circle a deer.

"Tell me about the murders, Jackson," said Harvey. "Tell

me how it made *you* feel."

Jackson didn't reply.

"I don't have time to play games, Jackson. How did it feel to burn the limbs off someone?"

No reply. Instead, Jackson just struggled against the chain.

"How will your wife feel when she finds out who the killer was?"

"No," said Jackson. "*She* can never know."

"Detective Chief Inspector Harris," said Harvey, "would you agree that you've found the man you're looking for?"

There was short silence, and then a weak voice from the far side of the small C-shaped clearing spoke. "That's fair to say," he said. "But I don't think it matters anymore, does it?"

"Oh it matters, Harris," said Harvey. "Jackson, tell Harris about how you glued Noah Finn to the bathtub."

"No," said Jackson. His voice suddenly broke. "I'll deny it all."

"You probably won't get a chance, Jackson. But if there's one thing I've learned in life, it's that people always feel better after a confession."

Harvey began to pace again in a wide circle. He stopped with his back to the fire and looked out over what was once the grounds where he and his sister had played when they were young.

"I've encouraged many confessions, Jackson. It's what I do best. I enjoy retribution. I can't help it. I'm not sick or twisted, and I'm certainly not the psychopath you say I am."

He turned again to face Jackson.

"I just enjoy seeing people get what they deserve."

He nodded into the darkness among the trees, and the chain links slowly began to pay out. Jackson began to lower.

"No, stop. Harvey, *no*."

"Don't fight it, Jackson. All you have to do is tell us."

"Harvey stop, you sick bastard."

Jackson's toes dipped briefly into the scalding hot water. He fought to keep his tired legs bent and away from the heat.

"Are you ready to talk, Jackson?"

Harvey's face was emotionless.

Jackson's face was a picture of perfect misery.

He began to sob.

"Tears won't help you, Jackson," said Harvey. "You've been a very bad man. The only thing that might help you now is a confession."

"I can't. It was a blur," sobbed Jackson. "I wasn't thinking straight."

"What was a blur? Was it cutting Noah Finn's nuts off and stuffing them in his mouth? Or was it slicing his stomach open and letting his guts fall into his lap in front of his waking eyes?"

Harvey paced once more.

"Which was it? Perhaps it was the pinning somebody down with stakes through their wrists and ankles, and letting them drown in their own blood? Maybe *that* was the blur? What do you think?"

Harvey nodded into the trees again, and slowly, a few more links of chain rolled across the thick branch above.

Jackson's feet sank into the scalding water.

He began to holler and growl, deep, carnal and angry. More chain was released and Jackson's feet hit the sides of the red-hot copper tub. His ankles began to blister as they succumbed to the vicious hiss and sting of the boiling water. The growl became a shrill scream.

"Ready to tell us about it, Jackson?" said Harvey. "The longer you take, the harder it'll be. But confess, and I'll make it as quick as possible."

"No Harvey," said Melody. "Stop. He's had enough. Let the law deal with him."

She tried to stand, but could only manage to get to her knees.

"You're innocent, Harvey. Stop and all this will be over."

Harvey offered her a smile.

"Last chance, Jackson," he said.

Jackson continued to sob and mumble apologies aimed at nobody.

"I'm sorry. I'm so sorry. It was the only way."

"Then it's over," said Harvey. "Goodbye, Jackson."

Harvey turned to the trees.

"Shaun?" he called.

Shaun Tyson appeared at the edge of the darkness.

"Are you ready for your new beginning?" asked Harvey.

Shaun nodded.

"Are you ready to leave the weak and perverted mind of the old Shaun Tyson behind?"

Shaun nodded once more.

"Say it, Shaun," said Harvey. "Tell me you're a new man. Show me how strong you are."

"I'm strong," said Shaun, a little weaker than he'd hoped.

"Louder, Shaun."

"I'm strong."

"Louder. I want you to feel it when you say it."

"I'm strong," yelled Shaun. "I'm strong."

"Are you weak?" asked Harvey.

"No," said Shaun.

"I can't hear you, Shaun."

"No," shouted Shaun.

"Are you perverted?"

"*No*." Shaun's face had reddened from the shouting and his windpipe stuck from his neck.

"Are you a new man, Shaun?"

"Yes."

"Then show me," said Harvey.

Without hesitation, Shaun cast the end of the chain away. It ran freely over the thick branch above, and Jackson landed with a splash into the searing water. His scream seemed to pierce the very darkness around them. His thrashes sent the boiling water onto the hot coals, which sent up clouds of steam that partially hid the horrific death.

The chain fell down on top of Jackson. He thrashed from left to right, unable to stop the pain from biting every nerve in his body. He flung his bound hands out over the edge to pull himself out, but the scorching copper seared his skin, melting it, so he simply slid back inside from the inescapable agony.

His visceral screams were lost to the trees and the dark night.

Melody turned away and held Boon with her bound hands, who grew excited at the commotion.

"Harvey, get him out," she said. "Enough is enough."

Harvey didn't reply.

He stepped over to Melody, and once more, bent down beside her.

"What have you done, Harvey?" she whispered, in disbelief at what she'd seen.

"I finished it," replied Harvey. "Once and for all."

"But you were innocent," she said. "You could have walked."

The thrashing and splashing stopped with abrupt silence. There was just the sound of hissing coals and the searing hot water settling.

"I'm still innocent, Melody. Only not in your eyes. I was always guilty in your eyes, wasn't I?"

"No, Harvey. You changed, you-"

"I've always been me, Melody." He spoke softly. The time for violence and rage had passed, perhaps for good.

"I'm sorry," said Melody. "I'm sorry I doubted you. I'm-"

"Don't apologise, Melody. We had a good time, didn't we?"

He kissed her forehead and smoothed her hair for the last time.

"No, Harvey, don't go. It doesn't have to end like this," she whispered, pleading.

Harvey stepped away.

"Harvey, stop," she shouted.

Harvey didn't reply.

"Harvey, come back."

Harvey didn't reply.

"Harvey, *stop*," Melody shouted, then took a breath. "It doesn't have to end this way," she said softly to the empty night.

She paused.

"Harvey."

Harvey didn't reply.

Finding a hostel so late at night had been difficult. Shaun had to beg to be let inside, and then had paid double for the little room, which wasn't much to look at, but to Shaun, it was everything he'd dreamed of. Outside his little window, the rain fell hard, bouncing off the surface of the road and the parked cars. Headlights illuminated each drop as if they sparkled.

Shaun thought of his mum.

She'd be sitting in her kitchen at the little table they'd eaten so many breakfasts and dinners at before. She'd probably be smoking and cradling a cup of tea in her hands as she often did.

He wondered if she'd be crying. It was a question he'd asked himself when he'd been tied up in the back of the van, and when Harvey Stone had caught him in the forest. But this time, his mind was clear. His thoughts ran wild, with the freedom and innocence of a child.

She'd be okay. She'd be happy for him. He made a mental note to call her, just to hear her voice.

A group of people walked by his window, and he moved back away from the glass, but then stopped. He was allowed to look out of the window.

He was free now. Free to do as he pleased. Free to live his life.

Thanks to Harvey Stone.

Of all the men in all the world that might offer Shaun a second chance, Harvey Stone had been at the bottom of the list.

But the man had done something to Shaun. He'd awakened something inside him, something that he'd never had before, but had seen in other men.

A confidence.

Shaun emptied his rucksack onto his bed and separated his belongings. He folded his clothes neatly, and placed his wallet, passport and money carefully together. Then, while his freedom ran amok inside his new-born mind, he changed into his smart set of clothes. He ran some water into his hands and smoothed his hair then pulled his coat on. He pocketed his multi-tool, wallet and loose items. Then Shaun walked out into the hallway, locking the door to his room behind him.

The rain was hammering down, but he stepped onto the pavement of Amsterdam anyway, and let the water splash onto his face.

He smiled at how fresh it felt, the rain, the cold air, and freedom.

A man and a woman were standing beneath the canopy of a closed restaurant a few doors away. They argued in another language, French maybe or Italian; Shaun didn't know.

He ignored them and focused on his own joy.

How powerful he'd felt when he'd cast the chain away and let that man fall to his death. How in control he felt of his own destiny.

A loud slap caught Shaun's attention. He turned to see the man recoil from the blow the woman had delivered, in time to see him retaliate with a blow of his own.

Shaun stepped back into the doorway and out of sight.

The woman gave a cry, and even the loud rain couldn't hide the dull thuds of punches and kicks. Shaun had heard them on many occasions in prison. It was a noise he'd never forget. It wasn't like the sound of a punch in a movie; the sound of a real punch was unlike any other noise.

"Are you strong?" asked Harvey, a voice inside Shaun's head.

Shaun closed his eyes.

"Are you strong?" he asked again.

"Yes," Shaun whispered.

"Louder, Shaun," said Harvey. "Are you strong?"

"Yes."

"Are you in control?"

"Yes."

Shaun stepped from the doorway.

"Are you a new man?"

"Yes."

"Louder."

"*Yes*," shouted Shaun.

He began to walk towards the couple. The woman was on the wet ground, trying to scramble away from the man. Her dress had pulled up from the struggle, and she was screaming.

"Are you a new man?"

"Yes," shouted Shaun.

The man bent over with his hand on the woman's throat.

"Are you strong?"

"Yes."

A silence seemed to fill Shaun's mind. The man landed a slap across the girls face, but the scene played out in slow motion.

"Are you a new man?" asked Harvey's voice.

"Yes," whispered Shaun. "But..."

Another slap sent the woman's face to one side. Her pleading eyes landed on Shaun's.

"But what, Shaun?"

"Am I ready?" he whispered.

Harvey didn't reply.

A NOTE FROM THE AUTHOR

Where better to end a huge chapter of Harvey's life than at the place where it all began? The house, where once upon a time a small boy saw the outline of a face in the moonlight and his world changed still stands, and next time I'm I'm in the UK, I'll pay it a visit.

Theydon Bois has been the centre of Harvey's world for a long time. The sleepy little village a few miles from London on the edge of Epping Forest was also the centre of my world. Although we lived a few miles away in Hornchurch, it seems most of my family lived in or around Theydon Bois and if we ever met up for family events, it would be in Theydon Bois.

My grandfather lived in the first house as you enter the village, my father had a house there, aunt and uncles, and countless others and I have great memories of well-kept gardens, coal-bunkers and the village green, not to mention sitting outside the Queen Vic pub on a Saturday afternoon with my brother, while the adults all made merry inside.

Although, in Harvey's world, the house is now gone, I don't think it'll be the last time Harvey goes to Theydon Bois, and if he does, I'm sure he'll leave his mark.

I hope you can join him on his next adventure, where we leave the rural countryside, orchards and farmhouses to venture back into the city where Harvey finds himself caught up in a very familiar world, in Stone Raid.

Thank you for reading.

J.D. Weston

To learn more about J.D. Weston

www.jdweston.com
john@jdweston.com

ALSO BY J.D.WESTON.

The Stone Cold Thriller Series.

Book 1 - Stone Cold.

Book 2 - Stone Fury

Book 3 - Stone Fall

Book 4 - Stone Rage

Book 5 - Stone Free

Book 6 - Stone Rush

Book 7 - Stone Game

Book 8 - Stone Raid

Book 9 - Stone Deep

Book 10 - Stone Fist

Novellas

Stone Breed

Stone Blood

The Alaskan Adventure

Where the Mountains Kiss the Sun

From the Ocean to the Stream

.

STONE COLD

Book One of the Stone Cold Thriller series

One priceless set of diamonds. Three of London's ruthless east end crime families. One very angry assassin with a hit list.

Harvey Stone has questions that someone will answer. Who killed his parents and why? Who raped and killed his sister? And why are his closest allies hiding the truth.

When Harvey is asked to kill east London's biggest crime boss in return for one name on his list, there is only one answer.

Can Harvey survive the gang war, untangle the web of deceit and uncover the truth behind his sisters death?

Stone Cold is the first book in the Stone Cold thriller series.

If you enjoy fast-paced adventure, gritty vigilante stories and no-nonsense heroes, then you'll love J.D. Weston's brand new Thriller Series.

STONE FURY

Book Two of the Stone Cold Thriller series

The lives of twelve young girls are being sold. The seller is on Harvey Stone's hit list.

When ex-hitman Harvey Stone learns of an human trafficking ring taking place in his old stomping ground, he is sickened. But when he learns the name of the person running the show, an opportunity arises to cross one more name of his list.

Can Harvey save the ill-fated girls, and serve justice to those who are most deserved?

Stone Fury is the second book in the Stone Cold thriller series.

If you enjoy fast-paced adventure, gritty vigilante stories and no-nonsense heroes, then you'll love J.D. Weston's brand new Thriller Series.

STONE FALL

Book Three of the Stone Cold Thriller series

One evil terrorist with a plan to change the face of London. One missing child, and one priceless jade Buddha. Only Harvey Stone and his team of organised crime specialists can prevent disaster.

When Harvey and the team intercept a heist to rob a priceless jade Buddha, little did they know they would be uncovering a terrorist attack on London's St Paul's Cathedral, and a shocking hostage scenario.

Can Harvey and the team stop the terrorists, save the little girl and rescue the priceless Buddha?

Stone Fall is the third book in the Stone Cold thriller series.

If you enjoy fast-paced adventure, gritty vigilante stories and no-nonsense heroes, then you'll love J.D. Weston's brand new Thriller Series.

STONE RAGE

Book Four of the Stone Cold Thriller series

Two of east London's most notorious gangs go head to head with the Albanian mafia, and one angry assassin who's out to clean up.

When Harvey Stone is sent undercover to put a stop a turf war between the Albanian mafia and two of East London's most notorious gangs, nobody expected him to be welcomed like a hero by an old face.

Has Harvey finally gone rogue, or will he put a stop to the bloodshed once and for all?

Stone Rage is the fourth book in the Stone Cold thriller series.
If you enjoy fast-paced adventure, gritty vigilante stories and no-nonsense heroes, then you'll love J.D. Weston's brand new Thriller Series.

STONE FREE

Book Five of the Stone Cold Thriller series

Death by internet. A mind blowing masterplan, where death holds all the cards.

Harvey Stone plays guardian angel on international soil when two governments prepare to do battle, and the lives of innocent people are at stake.

Can Harvey free the condemned women and avert an international disaster. Can he defy all odds and escape alive?

Find out in Stone Free, the fifth book in the Stone Cold Thriller series.

If you enjoy intense thrillers, with shocking storylines, then you'll love this new series from J.D. Weston.

STONE RUSH

Book Six of the Stone Cold Thriller series

Europe's slave trade is alive. MI6 is falling down, and Harvey Stone is caught in the middle.

Harvey yearns for the quiet life, but when a close friend is captured and tortured, and refugees become slaves, Harvey is forced out of retirement.

Can Harvey put a stop to the human traffickers and save the girls from a torturous death? Can he prevent the gang's devastating plans?

Find out, in Stone Rush, the sixth book in the Stone Cold Thriller series.

If you enjoy intense thrillers, with shocking storylines, then you'll love this new action crime thriller from J.D. Weston.

STONE GAME

Book Seven of the Stone Cold Thriller series

Tragedy strikes. A killer runs wild, and an old enemy raises the stakes.

Memories of Harvey's kills return to haunt his freedom. But as the body count grows and the past become reality, the hunter becomes the hunted.

Has Harvey gone back to his old ways? Is he destined for a life on the run?

Stone Game is the seventh book in J.D.Weston's Stone Cold Thriller series.

If you like your action hard and fast, with page-turning intensity, you'll love this series.

STONE RAID

Book Eight of the Stone Cold Thriller series

A pair of cursed diamonds. A brutal gang ran by evil twin brothers. And an ex-hitman who finds himself deep inside a Victorian legend.

When ex-hitman Harvey Stone emerges from laying low, he stumbles into a cruel and twisted plot devised by evil twin brothers to bring together two cursed diamonds, and unleash hell in London.

But the deeper Harvey delves into their plans, the more twisted they become, and saving the diamonds becomes his toughest challenge yet.

Can Harvey bring down the evil twins and prevent the cursed diamonds from destroying more lives? Can he find right from wrong in this twisted tale of lies and deceit?

STONE DEEP

Book Nine of the Stone Cold Thriller series

An ancient Spanish legacy. A shocking explosion in the City of London. And an ex-hitman fueled by revenge.

When ex-hitman, Harvey Stone is asked by an art collector, Smokey the Jew, to kidnap a member of a rival gang and extract details of a heist, little did he know the move would open the doors of hell and endanger everyone he cares for.

But renowned art thief, Dante Dumas will go to any length to find his family legacy, killing anyone who stands in his way.

Can Harvey survive Dante's devious plans, and can he find retribution for his lost love?

STONE FIST

Book Ten of the Stone Cold Thriller series

Two East London gangs. One ex-hitman clinging to the past. And a brutal fight to the death.

When ex-hitman Harvey Stone visits London to attend the wedding of one of his closest allies, he plans a visit to the grave of his long-dead mentor, Julios. But little does Harvey know that the trip will uncover a secret that will change his life forever and open doors to Harvey's past that have never before been revealed. But to forge an allegiance with a blast from Harvey's past he must first deal with a brutal death match between two rival gangs that threatens to wipe history from the face of the earth before it's even exposed.

ACKNOWLEDGMENTS

Authors are often portrayed as having very lonely work lives. There breeds a stereotypical image of reclusive authors talking only to their cat or dog and their editor, and living off cereal and brandy.

I beg to differ.

There is absolutely no way on the planet that this book could have been created to the standard it is without the help and support of Erica Bawden, Paul Weston, Danny Maguire, and Heather Draper. All of whom offered vital feedback during various drafts and supported me while I locked myself away and spoke to my imaginary dog, ate cereal and drank brandy.

The book was painstakingly edited by Ceri Savage, who continues to sit with me on Skype every week as we flesh out the series, and also threw in some amazing ideas.

To those named above, I am truly grateful.

J.D. Weston.

Printed in Great Britain
by Amazon